Sam dug his fingers into his scalp. "Sir, you've said in class that what makes this country different from most others is that here the accused is always presumed innocent until *proved* guilty."

"Out there"—Levine-Griffin waved toward the whole nation outside the window—"yes. But *here,* in this school, in this private school, we are not bound by so time-consuming a principle if we catch someone in fla-grante delicto. As has just happened, with the contra-band passing from one corrupt young man to another. Presumed *innocent*? How can that be when I—with my very own eyes—have come upon you immersed in your guilt? Reeking of your guilt!"

"Sir"—Sam looked up at Levine-Griffin and asked—"does this school have capital punishment?"

"Are you so hardened, young man, that you can joke at this moment when your future is in ruins?"

NAT HENTOFF is a well-known staff writer for *The Village Voice.* He is the author of *I'm Really Dragged but Nothing Gets Me Down, Jazz Country,* and *This School Is Driving Me Crazy* (to which *Does This School Have Capital Punishment?* is a sequel), all available in Dell Laurel-Leaf editions.

Does This School Have Capital Punishment?

NAT HENTOFF

LAUREL-LEAF BOOKS bring together under a single imprint outstanding works of fiction and nonfiction particularly suitable for young adult readers, both in and out of the classroom. Charles F. Reasoner, Professor Emeritus of Children's Literature and Reading, New York University, is consultant to this series.

Published by
Dell Publishing Co., Inc.
1 Dag Hammarskjold Plaza
New York, New York 10017

Lines from "Burnt Norton" in *Four Quartets* by T. S. Eliot used by permission of Harcourt Brace Jovanovich, Inc. and Faber and Faber Ltd.

Laurel-Leaf Library ® TM 766734,
Dell Publishing Co., Inc.

ISBN: 0-440-92070-1

RL: 6.4

Reprinted by arrangement with Delacorte Press
Printed in the United States of America
First Laurel-Leaf printing—April 1983

J
H

For all the readers of my previous novels
who have written me to question, criticize,
or ask for more stories.
And for Jo Jones.

I

"You're the new one." The headmaster's secretary looked at Sam as if the store had sent the wrong package. Actually, it was Sam's T-shirt that had frozen her attention. Blood-red over white, the swaying letters said:

DON'T CHEER, MEN. THE POOR
FELLOWS ARE DYING.

"Your mother let you go to school like that?" the thin woman, with thinner hair, asked.

"No'm." Sam caught his book bag just before it finished slipping off his shoulder onto the secretary's coffee mug. "When I left home, this was under another shirt, which is in my locker."

"Astonishing," said a large, round, blond man with a wispy beard who was leaning against the wall. "Everywhere, on the street, in the subway, in pizza parlors, and now even in the very headmaster's office of this school, people walk about with the

1

peculiar notion that other people wish to hear from their T-shirts. As for me, I have never met a T-shirt that had anything at all worth saying. Never. And yet the pity of it is they keep saying it incessantly. Very peculiar."

"Mr. Levine-Griffin," the secretary said crisply, looking at the round man while nodding toward Sam, "this is Sam Davidson. New boy. First year of high school. Under your command."

Levine-Griffin, director of the high school, held out his hand which Sam had barely touched before it was energetically withdrawn. "Welcome. I mean you, not your howling T-shirt. Sam, is it? Well, Sam, if you like to work and to keep stretching yourself, you'll have the time of your life here. Actually, this place will determine the whole rest of your life. It'll send you right into the power elite. After you've finished at the right college, of course.

"On the other hand"—Levine-Griffin frowned fiercely—"if you're shiftless and silly, you'll not last the term. And forevermore, from your tiny niche way down on the lower levels of society, you shall look up, in awe and envy, at all the boys who *did* graduate from Burr Academy."

"Duncan," the headmaster's secretary said, "you're going to terrify this child."

Levine-Griffin laughed. "Nonsense. This boy may be slovenly, but he doesn't seem to me to be fragile. Am I right, young man?"

2

Sam, figuring he was being made fun of but wasn't sure how, scowled. And said nothing.

"Well, Maggie," Levine-Griffin said to the secretary, "I must prepare a quiz for my first class."

"On the very first day, Duncan?"

"Best way to show right off who is master, and who is not."

As Levine-Griffin, humming a tune that seemed to have only one note, moved into the hallway, the humming suddenly stopped, and his mouth grew wide as, jamming himself against the wall, Levine-Griffin barely missed being run into by a short, stocky, alarmingly quick youngster who skidded to a stop in front of the secretary's desk.

"I *got* to see Mr. Monk, Miss Fitzgerald," the boy said, "I *got* to."

"Holmes," Levine-Griffin said in a shaky roar, "what is the meaning of this? You could have sent me to the hospital! And not even a 'Beg your pardon, sir.' It was as if I were not there at all. I am not accustomed to being treated as if I were not there, or here, or wherever I actually am. I *will* not be treated as if I do not exist."

Holmes turned and said, "Excuse me, sir, but this is an emergency, a terrible emergency." And he turned again to Miss Fitzgerald. "I *got* to see him."

The bony woman took off her glasses, cleaned them, put them on again, carefully poured herself a cup of coffee, and said, "Tell *me*."

3

"Got no time." Holmes was now hopping, first on one foot and then on the other.

"Tell *me*, dear boy," the secretary said coolly, "or remove yourself."

Holmes, in his agitation, was not so much hopping anymore as he was running in place. And breathing hard. "*He* said," Holmes broke into a swift chant, "that if I ever had to, really had to, pound somebody, I was to see *him* first. No matter what. Whether he was busy or not, I could see him right away. Well. Well, I am going to kill somebody. I am going to take somebody by the throat and bang his dumb head into the ground and stomp on him and grind his face into the dirt, and then I'm really going to mash him."

Sam, who had been watching with rapt attention, laughed, and could not stop laughing.

"What is so goddamn funny?" Holmes wheeled around and advanced toward Sam.

Sam held up his hand. "I know that feeling, that's all. You could be me, that's all. I mean, I could be you."

Holmes did not seem at all satisfied by this explanation but was distracted by Miss Fitzgerald speaking into an interoffice phone: "Emergency, Mr. Monk. Robert McLellan Holmes is about to start the school year with a homicide. He says you two have an agreement about such things." She listened, and nodded.

"All right, Rob. You may *walk* into Mr. Monk's office."

"And I," Levine-Griffin called after the boy as he headed toward the headmaster's door, "want to see you in *my* office at three to discuss the extra assignments I shall give you for turning these halls into the Indianapolis Speedway. Do you hear me, Holmes?"

His hand on the knob of the headmaster's door, Holmes mumbled, "Yes, sir." And then, very softly, said, "It would have been like running into mashed potatoes."

Sam snickered, to the glare of Miss Fitzgerald, but Holmes half-smiled at him as he went into the office.

II

His hair was gray, clipped short, and his eyes, steady and penetrating, were also gray. Tall, lean, Richard Monk looked, Sam thought, like an army officer. He held himself so damn straight, his clothes so neat and crisp. And he was looking straight at Sam's T-shirt.

"Do you know who said that?" the headmaster raised his eyes to Sam's.

"A guy named Jack Philip," Sam said. "He commanded a battleship during the Spanish-American War. At the Battle of Santiago, when the Spanish flagship just plain exploded, Philip's men began to cheer. And Philip, looking at the water full of dead people and dying people, said: 'Don't cheer, men. The poor fellows are dying.'"

"Is there a new line of historical T-shirts?" the headmaster asked.

"I had it made up myself," Sam answered warily. "I got others. Like, I Would Rather Be Right Than President. Henry Clay, you know."

"I know," said the headmaster. "You're a history buff?"

"Kind of, sir. American history." Sam began to relax. Too soon.

"I reluctantly allow T-shirts at Burr on very, very hot days. But not *speaking* T-shirts. Understood?"

Sam nodded.

"I always make it a point to visit with transfers." The headmaster rose and walked toward the window. "You have the student handbook, and I want you to read it very carefully. We do not tolerate dishonesty, cruelty, rudeness, aimlessness—or drugs. The possession or selling of any kind of drug, very much including marijuana, results in instant expulsion. The same with liquor. Whatever happens anywhere else in this society, the minds in *this* place will stay clear. I do not allow the students at Burr to be contaminated by these poisons, and I consider all of it poison.

"Now"—the headmaster had returned to his desk and picked up a folder—"I know your background. I can imagine the strain, during your first six grades, of being a student where your father is headmaster. It was wise to transfer, but this is your second transfer. Why did you leave the school you've been at the last two years?"

"My father said he made a mistake sending me there because it wasn't tough enough, they didn't give out enough work."

7

"He'll have no complaints on that score here."
Monk smiled. The smile made Sam feel like throwing up.

The headmaster glanced at the folder again. "Until the last year or so"—he looked at Sam—"you have had a history of being all too quick with your fists. I trust you've grown out of that."

Sam screwed up his nose. "I don't start anything, but I can finish anything somebody else starts."

"Well," the headmaster said, "for precaution's sake, I think I had better insist we enter into an agreement, similar to agreements I have with a few other rather inflammable students. I will not have fighting in the school. I simply will not have it. Anyone caught fighting is suspended. Therefore, if you are ever seized with an overwhelming urge to strike someone, you *must* come and see me first. No matter how outrageous the provocation has been. I shall make myself immediately available to you. Or, if I am out of the building, Mr. Levine-Griffin, director of the high school, will see you instantly."

The headmaster leaned toward Sam. "I know how hard it is to restrain yourself when the blood rises, but even if you are wholly convinced that you were the injured party and must fight back in self-respect, SEE ME FIRST OR YOU WILL BE SUSPENDED. Understood?"

"Sometimes there's no time at all, sir." Sam said, scratching his head.

"You are not an animal. You are not a robot. You will stop time."

"But what happens when I, like you said, stop time and see you?"

"If your case is just," the headmaster said, "the other student will be punished in an appropriate manner. The inmates do not run this asylum." Monk waited for a chuckle from Sam, but did not get one.

"Can I ask," said Sam, "what happened with the student who was just here? He said he had an agreement like that with you."

"Holmes, you mean. As I got the story from him, a few moments before he steamed in here, some other young men, high in spirits if not intelligence, decided to play catch with one of Holmes's books. A rare book of American Indian history, given him by his father. As Holmes rushed one of the passers, so to speak, the book was thrown wildly to a student coming along the street. He reached for it, dropped it, and trampled on it—by accident, I expect, though Holmes insists it was maliciously deliberate. Anyway, the book is a mess, pages torn, illustrations made filthy and crumpled. Holmes, though greatly motivated to pound, as he puts it, the inept pass receiver, stayed his hand and rushed here instead. Had he not, as he well knew, young Holmes would be on his way back home this very minute—under suspension. I shall now hear the other side, or sides, of the story, and decide on appropriate action."

Sam, completely identifying himself with Holmes, was shaking his head in wonder at that victim's self-restraint.

"What if you find out Holmes did tell you exactly what happened?"

The headmaster leaned back in his chair. "To begin with, those responsible will have to first try very hard to replace the book—in the same condition as it was before this morning's vandalism. Or, if they are unable to do that, they shall have to pay Holmes the book's full price which, since it is rare, will be considerable. As for further penalties, I do not reveal them in advance, but you can be sure that not one of those boys will ever again play games with someone else's property. I do not believe that any student found guilty here ever forgets the punishments I impose. Well"—the headmaster rose and held his hand out to Sam—"welcome to Burr."

Shaking the headmaster's hand, Sam found it cold. Very cold indeed.

III

Sam, walking down the corridor from the head-master's office, started whistling a low, sad tune he'd never heard before, but checked himself. Probably was against the law here. This was one school, damn it, where he was going to have a clean record. As he knew all too well, once you get a rep for breaking a school's silly rules, then you're the prime suspect for anything heavy that goes down—until you graduate, or get thrown out. Yes, sir, time for a fresh start. Going to memorize that student handbook and most of all, going to mind my own business.

"YOU—CAN'T—HIT—ME!" A high, cracking voice came around the corner. "YOU CAN'T HIT ME—OR YOU'LL BE SUSPENDED. SO GET AWAY FROM ME, HOLMES, OR I'LL TELL MR. MONK! MR. MON-N-N-N-K!"

A thin blond boy was backed up against the wall by Rob Holmes who, a foot shorter, was stretching a blunt fist to reach, not quite touch, the shrieker's nose. Watching, immobile, silent, were two other boys.

"If you don't shut up, Saddlefield"—Holmes was fiercely forcing himself to whisper—"I *will* get suspended and then, 'cause I'll have nothing to lose, I will take you by the neck and bang your rotten stinking head on the ground until it breaks. BREAKS, you understand. And I'll throw the pieces out the window so that your big-deal father, even with all his money, won't be able to get them put back together again. Now. Are you going to SHUT UP?"

Saddlefield, pressing himself against the wall so tightly that it was as if he were looking for a secret button that would open a secret door, nodded.

"Okay." Holmes was talking through his teeth. "That book you dropped and stomped on and turned into garbage meant a lot to me. A whole lot. Mr. Monk says you got to replace it or pay me what it cost. Well, you can't replace it. Guy who sold it to my father said that some minister out on the plains printed this Indian chief's story at his own expense, and ran out of money. This was the last known of the few copies that got made. So you won't be able to find another one. And I don't want your goddamn money. I want the *book*. And it's gone. So you're gonna pay me another way. I ain't gonna beat you up. I ain't even gonna spit on you.

12

But I'm gonna get you, Saddlefield, and there's no way you're gonna know how—until it's too late."

Holmes contemptuously flicked a finger at the blond boy and walked off. Saddlefield, hunching his shoulders, went in the opposite direction, keeping close to the wall.

"He wasn't the only one who screwed up that book," Sam said to the two Burr students who had been watching. "So why is it all coming down on him?"

One of the boys examined Sam. "New, huh? Whatever Saddlefield gets, he's got it coming. He's a sneak. The other guys who started it, well, you know, they didn't mean anything. But him! It's not just that he's the one who dropped the book and mangled it. The thing is, he's Saddlefield. You'll find out."

IV

"Do you have to take a lot of notes in this class?" Sam asked the tall, carrot-haired girl at the desk beside him. "I mean, does the grade depend on your giving her back exactly what she tells you, or can you think for yourself?"

The slender girl looked at Sam as if he were way across the room, or rather, as if *she* were way across the room. Raising her hand slowly, and then letting it drop even more slowly, she said, "Whatever."

"Whatever *what*?" Sam snapped.

"What's your name?" She looked at the T-shirt and giggled.

"Sam. Sam Davidson. Yours?"

"Rebecca. Rebecca—"

"Whatever," Sam finished for her, and grinned.

"It doesn't matter," Rebecca said. "Whatever you do, whether you take a lot of notes or a little, it doesn't matter. Nobody gets *A*s from Mrs. Wolf, and there aren't that many *B*s. Nobody knows how she grades and she won't tell and she's been here a hundred years and graduates come back to see her

14

to show off what they've become, and some, honest to God, bring their *children* to meet her. And you know what, if you ask me, she's a big pain in the ass."

"Well, now," a round black student with a deep hoarse voice interrupted, "Mrs. Wolf is no fool. My brother, he's an *expert* on fools. I mean, he thinks just about *everybody's* a fool, except me sometimes and that's because I have the benefit of being his brother, living with him and all. And it's true, you listen to my brother and he can show you the fool in everybody, even"—the boy paused for emphasis—"in *himself.* So Zeke's somebody you got to pay attention to in these things. And Zeke says if I don't take no other course in this turkey farm, I got to take Mrs. Wolf's because—"

"She's no fool," Sam said.

"Because," the black student persisted, "she's going to teach you how to *listen,* and that's the power you most need to make it through this world —knowing how to tell what people are *really* saying, not what they want you to think they're saying. You get it?"

"Yup," said Sam, "I'm no fool."

"That has yet to be proved," Rebecca said, placing a large, black leather, loose-leaf notebook on her desk, arranging alongside it three felt pens— blue, green, and red.

Sam waved at Rob Holmes, who had taken a seat

15

across the room, but Holmes, his fists still clenched, was staring at nothing with ferocious concentration.

Sam thought of going over to Holmes and asking him what grand torments he had in mind for Saddlefield, but remained in his seat. "Stay out of it," Sam said, half aloud. "Stay out of everything that's not your own business."

"Say what?" said the black student. "I'm Abner, by the way. Abner Williams."

"Sam. Sam Davidson." He stuck out his hand. "Just talking to myself, Abner. First sign of a fool."

"Not necessarily." Abner smiled. "Depends on what you're saying to yourself, depends on whether you're fooling yourself."

"Good morning, class!" Sam was startled. The deep, musical voice belonged to the tallest woman Sam had ever seen. Six feet, maybe more. She was dressed all in brown—blouse, skirt, shoes. And her skin was leathery. But what fascinated Sam was her hair—white, all white, falling in waves, past her shoulders down to her waist.

Her eyes were green, and as she slowly scanned the room, those eyes seemed to be piercing the innermost thoughts of each student. Her nose was aquiline, her face lean, but her mouth was wide and ready to smile. However, there was no telling what kind of a smile it would be.

"It will come as no surprise to you," she said, "that I am Mrs. Wolf. Emma Wolf. This course is called Oral History, although you will be doing a lot of writing. You will learn how to go back in time and connect what you find there with the present. And indeed, with the future as well."

She paused, took a long hand and brushed the white hair out of her eyes. "T. S. Eliot said it better:

" 'Time present and time past
　Are both perhaps present in time future,
　And time future contained in time past. . . .
　What might have been and what has been
　Point to one end, which is always present.'

"I want you all to think about that," Mrs. Wolf said. "Hard."

Thinking, Sam was also writing swiftly in his notebook. He tore out the page and handed it to Rebecca. The paper read, "If past and present are the future which already was, then everybody is presently out to lunch."

Rebecca, trying to suppress laughter, snorted, and instantly pushed the note back to Sam.

Mrs. Wolf gave them both a scornful, glacial look. "Since this is the first day of class, and you are not yet accustomed to my requirements," she said, "I shall not confiscate whatever that pitiful attempt at wit is. Also, I shall try to forget who, so to speak, created it; and who thought it so irresistibly comical that she disrupted the class with her charming grunts of laughter. I shall try to forget, but I shall not try very hard.

"Now"—Mrs. Wolf looked past Sam and Rebecca—"this course is one of the very few at Burr that requires you to go *outside* the school for much of your work. What kind of work are we talking about? In this course you will learn what it is to be an adult. And don't tell me you know, because you don't. Not one of you has the faintest idea."

Mrs. Wolf perched on the edge of her desk, looking like a splendid figurehead, once part of a magnificent ship that, except for her, was no more.

"People of your age are limited—in their *direct* knowledge of adults—to parents, relatives, teachers. And, to a much lesser extent, headmasters, custodians, storekeepers, et al. Therefore, you are ignorant of the real world. Terribly ignorant. It is as if you have spent all of your lives so far in a tiny children's village. Oh, to be sure, you *think* you know what adults do outside your children's village through what you see of them on television and in movies, books, and magazines. But most of that is secondhand, distorted, and only on the surface anyway.

"Think about it." Mrs. Wolf pointed a long finger at the class and at all students everywhere. "What do you *know* of the choices, the pressures, the triumphs, the crashing failures, and then the going up the mountain again—of being an adult? What

18

do you know of what adults *do*, except for those professions and vocations in which your parents are involved? And you probably know very little that is specific about these either. What do you know of *why* adults do what they do for a living? Beyond the money part of it? And what it was they wanted to do when they were your age, and did they ever get there? And, when they're sixty and seventy and eighty, what they think about where they've been all these years and what it all came to."

Sam had leaned forward, watching Mrs. Wolf intently. Excited, curious, he was also kind of afraid of getting into the life of some old stranger. And anyway, how was it to be done?

"Now"—Mrs. Wolf brushed the hair out of her eyes again—"within the next week, each of you will select, with my advice and consent, a *subject*. The subject will have to be at least sixty years old, and there is, of course, no upward limit. Relatives are not permitted, but otherwise, there are no restrictions as to line of work or, needless to say, race, sex, or religion."

If it's "needless to say," Sam was thinking, why say it? But he himself said nothing.

"Those of you"—Mrs. Wolf was now pacing the room—"with strong interests in a particular field will, I would think, search out someone who has spent his or her life in that field. If you're much involved in music, for instance, you might look for a symphony musician or a composer or an opera singer. Jazz, too," she said doubtfully. "I don't know about rock. There can hardly be any active, or retired rockers, for that matter, who are past sixty." Mrs. Wolf erupted in a short, derisive laugh. "What a bizarre image!"

"But if there was a rock musician in that age," Sam said, "it seems to me he'd have a lot to say about why he did what he did, and what he got out of it."

Mrs. Wolf looked at Sam, and nodded. "Okay. Maybe. If you can get one who can talk. Anyway, we shall go on, in the classes ahead, to explore interviewing techniques, research techniques, the required form for your final report on your subject, and the various interim reports I shall require to see how you're getting on. Remember, there are no limitations. Sports, police work, politics. What we are after is an *in depth* study, an understanding of the life and times of someone who has *lived* quite a while, whether wisely or not, and is still trying to. Any questions?"

"What if we can't find anyone who'll agree to be interviewed?" Rebecca asked.

"Then you'll get an *F*. Any hard questions?"

V

A few days later, rushing from the rain, a cheerful swarm of Burr Academy students invaded the subway station. Sprinting to catch the train roaring in, they barely stopped long enough to hold up their subway passes for the wooden-faced woman in the change booth.

If she had actually taken the time to examine the legitimacy of each pass, and the bearer thereof, there would have been a long bottleneck—thereby inconveniencing and greatly exasperating those adult citizens waiting behind the gaggle of youngsters to buy tokens.

But Transit Officer Felipe Cruz, standing to the side of the booth, was under orders to make spot checks of the swift students—in order to catch stray thieves in the act and also to deter those planning to defraud the Transit Authority at some future crowded moment.

At the top of the stairs, Sam had set his knapsack down—noting angrily that the books were soaking wet because he had forgotten to close it—and searched through his pockets for the subway pass. Finally, he found it in his shoe, where he had put it that morning in case he might get mugged at this subway stop which was still new to him. Picking up his knapsack, bottom side up, Sam watched, in acute disgust, as his books slithered down the stairs. By the time he had collected them all, the other Burr students were long gone, and Officer Cruz had ample leisure to examine this straggler.

"Your pass?" he said to Sam.

Sam took it from between his teeth and handed it to Officer Cruz, who took it gingerly. "How do I know what else you got in your mouth?" he said sourly as he looked at the pass. "Your name is Benjamin Bloom?"

"Oh, God!" Sam hit himself on the head. "I forgot! Listen, Benjy Bloom is a friend of mine, and he borrowed my subway pass and he lost it and so when he found his, he gave it to me."

"This pass"—Officer Cruz looked at it again—"expired last June. So, you are using a pass which is not yours—these passes are *not* transferable—and you are using a pass which is no longer valid. You have broken *two* regulations. You are a double delinquent."

"Aw look"—Sam was shaking his head in despair—"I didn't even think about needing a new pass. I just started at this new school. Wait, I remember,

I was supposed to see about getting a new pass but I had so many other things to get settled so I wouldn't get into trouble, and I didn't want to get in trouble right off in this new school, so I just forgot about the pass, you know, I mean I wasn't trying to get away with anything, I just *forgot*, damn it!"

Officer Cruz bristled. "Don't you swear at me! You're such a smart-ass, you can come down with me to headquarters and I'll book you as a juvenile offender."

"I wasn't swearing at *you!*" Sam wailed even more desperately. "I was swearing at *me*, at all the goddamn trouble I get into for no *reason*."

Cruz let himself smile a little. "You think about it, you'll find the reason." The officer took from his back pocket a long black notebook, thick with official-looking forms. Peeling off one of them, he began to fill it out.

Sam bit his lip, shook his head, and asked, "What's *that* for?"

"A summons," Officer Cruz said matter-of-factly. "You will have to appear in court, nine in the morning, two weeks from today, to answer the charge of subway trespass—which means you weren't entitled to use this pass which wasn't usable in the first place. The judge will decide the penalty. Unless"—Officer Cruz smiled broadly—"you can talk him out of it, which is as likely as me being the starting pitcher for the Yankees today." Cruz was much amused at the analogy. "Yes, sir, maybe I will pitch a no-hit game today."

Sam, looking at, but not seeing, the ground, was shaking his head again. "Terrific. I'm going to have to ask for time off from school to appear in court as a *criminal*. That'll really set me up at Burr. You might as well," Sam said bitterly, "put the cuffs on."

"You're going to learn something," Cruz said coolly. "You're going to learn something they should have taught you in that school of yours. You're going to learn to watch what you're doing— at all times. Okay, I need your name and address. And no funny business. Give me identification. Real identification."

Sam slowly pulled a battered wallet out of his knapsack and handed him the Burr identification card—with his picture on it.

Cruz compared the desolate boy in front of him with the truculent boy in the picture, wrote down the name, got his home address from Sam, handed him a summons, and kept a copy of it for the fat black notebook.

"Can I go now?" Sam said heavily.

"Why not?" Officer Cruz shrugged. "Unless you're going to play some other dumb trick."

Sam put his hand in his pants pocket, and then desperately, in his other pants pocket, and then in all his jacket pockets, and then dove into his knapsack. "Oh God," he said, "I don't have any money."

"Don't look at me," said Officer Cruz. "I'm not the Welfare. How far you got to go?"

"Seventy-two blocks. I live on Twelfth Street and Fifth Avenue."

"Jog," said Officer Cruz. "It won't take no time."

VI

As Sam took his seat at the dinner table, his mother had a chill of foreboding. Instead of his customary leap into his chair as he simultaneously lunged for two or more rolls, Sam sat down slowly and started tapping, tapping a spoon against a water glass. Though not loud, the sound's persistent dreariness seemed to echo from every corner of the room. The ceiling, too.

"Yegods!"—Sam's father looked up from a folder of reports in which he had been absorbed—"are things *that* bad at Burr?"

"Nope," Sam mumbled. "I'm doing okay."

"Then *what*?" his mother said. "What's wrong?"

"I got to go to court," her son said to his dinner plate.

"COURT!" his parents responded in a spiraling duet, the mother's shocked soprano intertwining with his father's skidding baritone.

Sam explained his double delinquency on the subway and, from his pocket, took the crumpled summons which his father—grumbling at the certain people's wilful inability to take proper care of even important documents—carefully unfolded. And read. And passed to his wife.

"Well," she sighed, "it says you can have a lawyer represent you."

"I don't need a lawyer." Sam was still talking to the dinner plate.

"For once he's right," Mr. Davidson said. "He doesn't need a lawyer because he's going to plead guilty. He'll be fined, which will come out of his allowance, and that'll be the end of it. It won't be on his record."

"Still," Mrs. Davidson said, "he'll need somebody. I'll go down with you, Sam."

"No!" Sam said glumly but firmly. "I don't need anybody."

"He's right again." Mr. Davidson looked at his wife. "It's cut-and-dried."

"I don't know why I should plead guilty though." Sam's voice was beginning to take on some of its normal combativeness. "I wasn't trying to cheat anybody. I'm entitled to a subway pass. I just didn't have the right one. And that's what I'm going to tell the judge."

"Pay the two dollars," said his father. "If you're worried about the money, I'll give you the money. You cannot win fighting something like this. I mean, if it were a matter of principle, you'd *have* to fight out of self-respect. But where's the self-respect when this all happened because you were your usual careless, babyish self? What are you going to say, 'Judge, I'm a hopeless slob, so it wasn't my fault'? Don't you realize that if you don't plead guilty—and you are guilty—you'll have to go to trial? Then you *will* need a lawyer who will have *no* defense for you except, 'This child shouldn't be allowed on the streets by himself.' It doesn't matter whether you *intended* to defraud the Transit Authority or not. You violated the regulations. You were trying to use a pass that wasn't yours. A pass that was out of date besides. Don't be stupid. Just go down and pay the fine. I'll call Mr. Monk and tell him what happened. It won't go against you at school."

"No." Sam shook his head. "I appreciate your being willing to do that, but I've got to handle this myself."

"I have to respect that," his father said.

"And I got to think about whether I'll plead guilty or not. Maybe I can plead guilty with an explanation and argue that the explanation really doesn't make me guilty at all."

"WHAT EXPLANATION?" his father roared. "That you're a yo-yo!"

"Carl," his wife said sharply, "you're being of no help at all."

"Sometimes," her husband grumbled, "I think this boy is beyond help."

28

"Bite your tongue," Mrs. Davidson said. "You know very well what real troubles boys can get into —troubles that can follow them all their days. So you have one hell of a nerve talking that way about this child. You don't appreciate this child."

Becomingly, Sam lowered his head in modesty until he was suddenly seized with a yearning for a handful of rolls, and snatched them from the center of the table.

His father sighed. "Of course, you're not a bad boy, let alone a wicked boy. But damn it, Sam, you ought to be in the *Guinness Book of World Records* for being the most *irritating,* fundamentally decent boy there is."

"Gee," said Sam, "that's the nicest thing you've said to me in a long time."

Two hours later Mr. Davidson knocked on the door of his son's room. The record player was on so loud that he had to knock twice more, each time louder.

When Sam opened the door, his father motioned fiercely for the machine to be shut off. With obvious reluctance, Sam complied. "I thought," his father said, "there were to be no records, no radio, while you were doing homework."

"I did my homework. In study period."

"Then why," his father said in triumphant accusation, "did you bring books home?"

"They haven't fixed the lock on my locker yet. I didn't want to take a chance on leaving them there."

"Well, if your grades fall below what they ought to be in any subject, there'll be no records and no radio until they're back up again. Regardless of whether or not you say you've done your work in study period. If you're behind, you should be doing more studying here. But that isn't why I came in. You asked me about Major Kelley, that jazz musician I knew when I was going to school. Well, I found out he's still alive and still playing. He must be about sixty or sixty-five now. He could be a good subject for that project of yours. But you know, I had no idea you were that interested in jazz. You never play any of my old jazz."

"You said, and you said it a lot, that I should keep my butterfingers off those seventy-eights because I'd be sure to break them, and you can't get them anymore."

"So I did," his father said. "But I never hear jazz coming from this room. Just awful shrieks and whines and pounding, pounding."

"Oh, once in a while, I listen to the jazz stations," Sam said. "I've heard some of Major Kelley's old records on one of those shows. That's where I got the idea of maybe doing him for school. His trumpet kind of got to me. It stays in your mind."

"Here." Mr. Davidson took a folded piece of paper from his pocket. "This is where Kelley lives. It's in Greenwich Village, but way west of where we are. He's practically on the Hudson River. Phone number's there, too."

Sam's father sat down on the bed, filled his pipe, lit it, and said: "When I was in my last year of high school and then in college, I couldn't stay away from Fifty-second Street. There was one jazz club after another on that street; during the same night, you could hear Billie Holiday, Dizzy Gillespie, Art Tatum, Coleman Hawkins—and Major Kelley. I'd cram all my studying in during the day and early evening—I'd even read while I walked—so I could stay on the street at night. But it cost money and I didn't have much, so I'd usually try to hear what I could from the sidewalk. Until Major noticed me hanging around and got me into the clubs he was playing by saying I was his publicity man.

"That's what he'd tell people: 'This young cat, he's going to make me world famous, he's so sharp.' It got embarrassing because some of the other musicians believed him and wanted to pay me money to do for them what they thought I was doing for Kelley. But I wasn't doing a thing for Kelley. Newspaper columnists wrote about him because there was no one else like him—what he played, what he said, the way he dressed. Anyway, Major saved me by telling the other musicians I was working *exclusively* for him. So I was able to keep coming in for free."

"What made him so different?" Sam asked.

"I think you ought to find that out for yourself. You should see him fresh, not through your old man's memories."

VII

Richard Monk stood at the window, watching the students coming down the long street toward the tall, crisp red-brick building that was their last home-based harbor before college—and then the open sea. A few of the youngsters were walking, more or less purposefully, by themselves. Most, however, approached another day at Burr Academy in twos or threes, laughing, or appearing to be trading confidences of a most urgent nature.

"It's a fascinating time of life to watch, and to be able to keep on watching," Burr's headmaster said, still looking out the window. "They can, and must, keep testing themselves; and that means taking risks which may have quite unsettling consequences. But they're still of an age where, if they fall, there's always somebody to catch them right away. Their parents. Or us. Often, we get there first because we see a lot more of them than their parents do."

"And sometimes they splatter to the ground anyway," said Duncan Levine-Griffin who was leaning back on the green leather couch next to the headmaster's spacious, burnished antique desk which had once, it was said, belonged to a nearly illiterate junk dealer of vast, dusty means who happened to have been headmaster Monk's grandfather.

"Yes," the headmaster said, "I've lost a few. In a way, it's been my failure when I've had to expel a youngster."

"But it doesn't go on *your* college record," Levine-Griffin said, deadpan.

"But if I listened to you"—Monk looked at the head of the high school—"I would have expelled more students than I have."

Levine-Griffin fingered his thin beard. "Oh, I'm not faulting you for throwing out bad apples. That's your responsibility to the other kids and to the other parents. When you find someone selling marijuana or cocaine, or when you catch a chronic cheat or thief, you have to root him out or he can pollute the whole school with his diseased character."

"He?" the headmaster smiled.

"Oh." Levine-Griffin waved his hand impatiently. "He or she. You don't have to instruct me about nonsexist pronouns. Not with my name. Amy would only agree to marry me if she could bring her own name along. That's how this Episcopalian became half a Levine. God knows if the tradition will hold among our children and grandchildren. If it does, some poor child will eventually be trailing eight names behind himherself like Spanish grandees.

Anyway, about bad apples, when a kid gets that rotten, there's nothing more we can do for him. This is not a state training school. And it's just sentimentality to say it's your failure or my failure or the rest of the faculty's when heshe has to get kicked out."

"You read me wrong," the headmaster said. "I'm not in the least sentimental. On the other hand, I'm not yet convinced of my infallibility. I commend to you, sir, what Oliver Cromwell said to the General Assembly of the Church of Scotland."

Levine-Griffin groaned. "I know, I know."

"Cromwell said," the headmaster persisted, " 'I beseech you in the bowels of Christ, think it possible you may be mistaken.' "

"Do you think you've ever been mistaken in expelling a student?"

"No-o-o. But that's because—unlike you and the Queen of Hearts—I don't have people's heads cut off before I hear the evidence. Anyway, enough of crime and punishment. What do you make of young Davidson so far?"

"Bright enough, spectacularly disorganized, not very sociable. Holmes seems to be the only real friend he's made, and that's like being the buddy of a volcano. Also, Sam seems surly much of the time. Defiant by nature, I'd say, and that makes for a very prickly boy. Not my favorite type."

"It may look that way," the headmaster said, "but

I think what's really going on is that Davidson is trying very hard to stay in control of himself and not get that outlaw rep he had in both his previous schools. It's the strain of constant virtue that makes him seem surly."

"Maybe," said Levine-Griffin with no conviction at all. "Another thing. A couple of his history papers have been almost brilliant. He can make extraordinary historical connections, some of them quite bizarre but a few so startlingly penetrating that I suspected briefly that he was plagiarizing. But then I realized that no published historian would dare take such risks with the past. *However,* I have never seen such slobbish spellings. There are mistakes no self-respecting sixth-grader would make. And that boy, although enrolled in this exceptionally distinguished secondary school, has no more notion of how to paragraph an essay or punctuate a sentence than if he had been brought up by wolves away from all humankind and had only just now been deposited by those wolves in this school."

"Do you think this exceptionally distinguished secondary school might possibly be able to do something about that?" the headmaster addressed Levine-Griffin.

"I have already sentenced Sam to remedial classes. Not without much obnoxious resistance. The boy tells me it's originality of expression that counts—not such piddling, niggling irrelevancies as correct spelling, punctuation, and paragraphing. '*Anyone* can spell,' that surly boy says, 'but how many original *thinkers* do you come across?'

"I informed him"—Levine-Griffin bristled at the memory—"that since we both agree that *anyone* can spell, his refusal to focus on this matter indicates deliberate contempt of the basic rules of communication in the world at large and specifically here. Thereby he is insulting every other member of this community of correct-spelling scholars. I further informed him—and this is what turned the trick—that if he did not apply himself to the remedial work, I would begin to display each and every one of his compositions on the bulletin board for the grand entertainment of his fellow students."

The headmaster laughed. "That beats caning stubborn students in the old days, doesn't it?"

"Of course it does," Levine-Griffin beamed. "It's so much more cruel."

VIII

Sam had started to dial Major Kelley's number several times, but had broken off because he didn't quite know what to say if Kelley answered.

It couldn't be: "Sir, I'm doing a project at school on old people, and since you're an old trumpet player . . ."

And it couldn't be: "Mr. Kelley, my name is Sam Davidson and I want to know what it's been like to be a black jazz musician for fifty years so I can write it up and maybe get an *A*."

Banging his hand on his knee, Sam winced, picked up the phone, and dialed again.

"Mr. Kelley?"

"Depends," said the brisk voice on the other end.

"Uh, my name is Sam Davidson. I'm in an advanced communications course in high school, and I would like to interview you about your—uh—long career."

There was a pause. "What you want to know?"

"Everything," said Sam. "I mean everything you'd care to tell me. How you started, whom you've played with, what it was like on Fifty-second Street with Billie Holiday, Coleman Hawkins, and Dizzy Gillespie."

"How do you know about Fifty-second Street?"

"My father used to hang out there when he was going to school."

"Uh-huh. Why you pick me?"

"My father told me about you."

"Uh-huh. So *you* don't know nothin' about me."

"I've heard some of your records."

"Which ones?"

Sam desperately tried to remember the titles. "I'm not sure what it was called, but one was a blues, a blues about being lost inside your head and not being able to find any way out."

Major Kelley laughed. "Yeah, that was 'Prisoner of the Blues.' The guy who was supposed to sing it never showed up. So that's how I made my vocal debut on records. Sold so well, maybe fourteen copies—I'm surprised you ever got to hear it—that I didn't sing again on records for fourteen more years. Well, I tell you what. We'll do an audition. I'm playing in Red Stovall's band on a Hudson Line boat this Sunday. Leaves at one o'clock from the Fiftieth Street pier. You introduce yourself, and we'll see if we're in the same groove. We'll see if we got anything to say to each other."

The Hudson Line boats were mainly for tourists who, wanting to get a clear sense of Manhattan as an island, spent a couple of hours in a watery circle around that densely packed center of the United States—or so its natives liked to think of it.

A guide, cracking brittle jokes and throwing in bits of semi-imaginary history, would discourse on the wonders and terrors of Manhattan through the boat's public address system until the visitors, delighted they were only visitors to fabled Gotham, could barely wait to get home—alive.

Occasionally, however, there was no guide, no jokes, no ghosts of victims of the insatiable muggers. On those afternoons, jazz took over one of the battered but sturdy and marvelously spacious boats. The route was the same, circling the asphalt island, but the commentary was by what black musicians in the South used to call "singing horns"—powered by a rhythm section which, though stationary, sounded as if it were strutting up and down the stairs, across the decks, and even out onto the water.

Sam, buying his ticket, noticed on a placard that two bands were booked for this trip: on the upper deck, Red Stovall and his Original New York Rhythm Kings; and two decks below, Hamilton LaCroix and his Inside-Outside Surprise Band. There was a photograph of Red Stovall seated at a piano—a round-faced, light-skinned, amiable-looking man who seemed to be in his fifties. Also on the placard was a shot of Hamilton LaCroix, a

40

young black trumpeter, maybe in his late twenties, who was built like a barrel, with the head of a highly suspicious, bad-tempered turtle. But nowhere was there any picture, or mention, of Major Kelley.

The chairs in front of the bandstand on the upper deck were rapidly being filled, but there was one empty seat at the edge of the front row, which Sam jumped into.

Red Stovall, eyes closed, smiling slightly, was warming up, playing a lean, loping blues in which the portly, brown-skinned bassist joined, nodding his head as if he were meeting an old, comfortable friend. The drummer, a spidery-looking man of indeterminate age, was still setting up his equipment which included—in addition to trap drums, cymbals, sticks, and brushes—a cluster of gongs and a slide whistle.

Seated on a folding chair near the piano was the clarinetist, a bearded white man in his forties, who was trying out reeds, sourly rejecting one after another until he found one that made him beam. And the robust youthful trombonist, red-haired, red-faced, grinning at a friend in the audience, was taking a long swig from a beer bottle. Sam couldn't help grinning himself because the musician reminded him of the Cowardly Lion in the old movie *The Wizard of Oz.*

Red Stovall looked up from his piano and said

softly but firmly to the trombonist, "We'd like you with us on the last set, you know. We'd miss you terribly, were you gone."

"Just beer, pops," the trombonist said.

"I remember a night in Hackensack," the leader continued just at softly and just as firmly, "when come midnight, we all looked around the stand and there was that slide trombone raring to go and nobody, just nobody, was there to pick it up. Poor thing just lay there, pining away."

"Okay, okay," said the trombonist, finishing the beer.

"And," Red Stovall persisted, in little more than a whisper, "we asked the bouncer if maybe he could find our missing lamb, and he did. Yes, he did. Out in the parking lot, hollering to the moon—in so many interesting keys. I never knew the blues had so many keys. And you were barking and carrying on with such words, what we could make out—why, I never knew you knew such words. Well, so we picked you up, and put you down, just like a leaking baby, in the car. And the last words you said to me—actually, you sang them so sweet—were, 'Just beer, pops. Just beer.' "

The trombonist shook his head and blew a long mournful note which ended, however, in a cheerful blare.

"A musician is a professional or he is just some mama's boy who never grew up. That's all there is to it. Nothing more need be said." This pronouncement, delivered in a slightly raspy, clipped voice, came from a wiry, balding man who had just come on the stand and who could not have been more gleamingly neat—from what was left of his hair to his precisely trimmed mustache to his carefully orchestrated, crisply clean and pressed clothes. He wore a blue blazer of the quality and conservative cut Sam had thought was exclusive to headmasters; a light blue shirt with French cuffs; a dark red silk tie; and gray flannel slacks.

"Hey, Major," Red Stovall smiled broadly. The newcomer magisterially acknowledged the greeting, took his trumpet out of an expensive-looking, deep-brown leather bag, tuned up, sat down alongside the clarinetist, looked at Sam, looked at him again, this time carefully, consulted his watch, and looked at Red Stovall. The leader nodded and, stomping out the brisk tempo, Stovall began the set with "At the Jazz Band Ball"—the three horns standing as they soared through the first chorus.

Major Kelley took the lead, lining out the bold, leaping melody with a big, biting tone while the clarinet wove in and out of Kelley's lines, his sound like hot spice. The trombonist took the low road, punctuating everything else going on with long smears, roars, roller-coaster slides, and what sometimes sounded to Sam like maniacal laughter. Behind the horns, the rhythm section kept a crackling, driving beat, with the spidery drummer seeming to have four hands and maybe three feet.

After the opening ensemble, the first solo was Major Kelley's. His trumpet angled toward the sky, Kelley took the melody, stated it with silvery simplicity, and then began to transform it—bending and curving the tune so that it seemed to be many tunes, but always there was enough of a glimpse of the original theme for Sam to be able to follow the astonishing things that were happening to it. He had, to be sure, listened to jazz recordings, but this was the first live jazz Sam had experienced; and the full force of the music, seen as well as heard, so overwhelmed him that he absorbed it with his mouth wide open, as if his eyes and ears were not enough to hold it all.

Major Kelley, lowering his trumpet at the end of the solo, looked at the stunned boy, smiled slightly, and nodded. Without sound, his lips said, "Come up after the set."

IX

"I was watching you," Major Kelley said to Sam who stood next to the stand while the rest of the crowd was moving to the lower deck and Hamilton LaCroix's Inside-Outside Surprise Band. "Best of all things in this life, next to playing itself"— Kelley carefully put his trumpet in the brown leather bag—"is seeing someone open himself to the music.

"I've been in places where it seemed nobody was listening at all. Everybody talking loud and smoking and drinking, and you wondered why you were there at all. They didn't *need* any music. You could have played junk and they wouldn't have known the difference because they were just hearing themselves. That's a real stone drag, boy, when you're playing your own *life*—because that's what this music is, our own selves, everything we've been and seen and lost and won and lost again—and nobody's paying any mind. But if you see one face out there that's digging it, that's listening so hard it would take an earthquake to break the connection, why, all the rest of those people acting like they've been brought up in a barnyard don't count anymore. So long as there's one face all lit up, nothing more need be said.

"Not that you were the only one today, boy"— Kelley checked to see if his tie were straight—"but it's a real pleasure when it's a young face that understands. Because as old as some of us are, the music keeps us young, so youngsters are our natural audience. Now, no point your doing your interview here. Not enough time between sets and besides, it should be done where it's calm so my memory can ease itself back into the past like the waves going out, slow and steady, on a quiet beach. Here's my address."

Major Kelley handed Sam a small white card on which was printed, in raised black letters, his name, address, phone number, and at the bottom:

MASTER TRUMPETER
AVAILABLE FOR ALL OCCASIONS
ADVANCE DEPOSIT REQUIRED—
EXCEPT FOR PRESIDENTIAL AND
OTHER CIVIC CEREMONIES

Only Freshly Tuned Pianos Will Be Acceptable

"How about next Saturday?" Major Kelley said. "Early, like noon."

"That's early?" Sam asked.

"For a musician it is, boy. Now, let's go downstairs and hear this LaCroix cat. I've been hearing *about* him, but I never got to catch him live. You know, this music never stops changing and if you don't keep up with it, it won't wait for you. I don't mean you got to change the *fundamental* way you play, but you got to know what's going on and maybe, just maybe, you'll find a few new things that fit naturally into your own stuff. I mean, from the time I became a pro, when I was nineteen or so, I always had a style you couldn't mistake for no one else's, but just like I kept moving along, *it* kept moving along. You understand me, boy?"

"I think so," Sam nodded. "It's like you said. If what you play is your life, it can't ever be exactly the same."

"You got it." Major Kelley started down the stairs. "Nothing more need be said."

On the stairs, before he could see Hamilton La-Croix, Sam heard the trumpeter playing so fast that if he hadn't known the music was live, he would have thought that somebody had taken a 33⅓-rpm record and speeded it up to a 78. Yet, incredibly swift as the music was, each note flew clean and clear, the long lines connecting them snapping like a whip in the river air.

"That boy has some chops," Major Kelley said appreciatively.

Sam looked puzzled.

"Technique," said Kelley. "He's got the strength and control in his lips, his fingers, his mind, to play everything he hears, and man, he has got big ears."

Standing beside LaCroix was a young, thin, short tenor saxophonist whose sound, Sam thought, was twice as big as he was. And the rhythm section, also in their mid and late twenties, played hard and loud, the intensity of their swinging at odd variance with their expressionless faces.

When the first number was over, LaCroix, seeing Major Kelley, made a slight bow in his direction.

"He knows you," Sam said.

"He'd better, him being a trumpeter," Kelley said softly as he bowed slightly in turn. "I'm part of what he came out of."

"I want to introduce"—LaCroix spoke whisperingly into the microphone—"one of the great legends of jazz, a man who, along with Louis Armstrong, Roy Eldridge, and Dizzy Gillespie, is the reason us younger musicians are here at all. He was one of those who laid down the foundation. Ladies and gentlemen, my musical grandfather, Major Kelley!"

"Father will do," Kelley growled.

"There he is," said LaCroix, pointing to Kelley. "He's playing upstairs with Red Stovall this afternoon and now, I most sincerely hope, he'll play a number with us down here."

Major Kelley moved onto the stand at a jaunty,

unhurried pace, removed his trumpet from the deep-brown leather bag (which LaCroix eyed with admiration), and nodded again to the leader.

"You call it, brother," LaCroix said. "Anything you want. Any key. And you beat it off."

Kelley smiled thinly. "You are very hospitable, young man, but this is your gig, and I'll fit in somehow with whatever you usually do."

LaCroix rubbed his nose in momentary indecision.

"Don't worry, young man," Major Kelley said coolly, "there's no way you can embarrass me."

LaCroix pressed his lips together, stared at Kelley, and heard the closed-faced tenor saxophonist behind him mutter: "Do what he says, Ham. He ain't in a wheelchair, you know." The saxophone player laughed, not unkindly.

LaCroix shrugged and announced "Black Sunlight." Instantly, the band zoomed into a blazingly fast theme that spiraled up and up and then plunged steeply downward, as if into an elevator shaft. For a while, Major Kelley just listened, his trumpet at his side, and then suddenly, he joined in with a bright skipping countermelody that wittily moved in and out of the other musicians' lines. Despite the breakneck speed of the tempo, Kelley had no trouble keeping up—except that unlike the dense bursts of sound exploding from LaCroix and the tenor saxophonist, Kelley's playing was spare. For every seven or eight notes they played, he judiciously selected one of his own. And because of the space he left between his notes, Kelley's melodies were clearer, more singing, more dancing.

So too in the solos, Hamilton LaCroix's was brilliant. Even a novice listener like Sam could tell that. LaCroix ranged all over the trumpet and indeed seemed to stretch it—high and low—beyond what any brass horn had ever been asked to do before. There were so many notes coming so fast that Sam wondered how LaCroix was able to think up all of them, let alone get each one out of the horn with such precise clarity.

Major Kelley, listening intently to the younger trumpeter but not watching him—looking out instead toward the river—then started his own solo with just a fragment of a fiendishly complex melodic line that LaCroix had ended with. Kelley first played that fragment as if he were holding it up to the light for all to see—like a magician before he starts a trick. Softly, taking his time and swinging all the while, the elderly trumpeter turned that miniature melody inside out and upside down before putting it back into its original shape. At that point, Kelley began building that fragment into a brand-new design of much larger dimensions—still open, airborne, and, Sam thought, full of sunlight.

When the number was over, as the crowd applauded, Hamilton LaCroix, pointing to Major

Kelley, himself started applauding, as did the rest of the band. Kelley bowed, his face impassive, except for his eyes, which shone. Sam stood, banging his hands together, and then others in the crowd rose until there was a standing ovation for Kelley.

"You cut me on my own turf," LaCroix said to the older man with awe. "God knows what you'd do to me if we were both playing *your* stuff!"

"I just surprised you a little," Major Kelley said. "I wouldn't call it cutting. We'd have to spend a whole night playing together before we could really add up the score."

"I'd like that, Mr. Kelley. I figure it would be a real education, no matter how it came out."

"Well"—Kelley was putting his trumpet back into the leather bag—"we'd both be in excellent company. My sense of you, young man, is that you understand the profound wisdom of Casey Stengel when he said, 'They say it can't be done, but that don't always work.'"

X

Sam woke early, about six, tried to go back to sleep, but couldn't. There was music in his head. So he washed, dressed, grabbed a handful of Fig Newtons, and took a Coke out of the refrigerator—but not without first listening hard to make sure he wasn't going to get caught by some parent also up too early.

Although the doors of Burr Academy were not unlocked until seven fifteen, Sam decided to be—for the first time in his life—not only early for school but the very first one there.

Walking rather proudly down the street to Burr a little before seven, Sam was much annoyed to see the back of another boy already at the gates, reading. As he got closer, Sam saw it was Rob Holmes, and wasn't annoyed at all.

"I'm always the first one," Rob said, closing his book. "I gotta get out of the house before anybody else is up."

"How come?" Sam leaned against the gate.

"Soon as my father opens his eyes, he starts yelling. He yells at whatever he sees—me, the dog, my mother, my sister. He's so used to yelling, he doesn't know he's yelling. Inside the house, I mean. Outside, that's a whole other story. Outside, he talks so soft that people think nothing could *ever* get him mad. That's what my mother says they think. I don't believe it myself. But anyway, when the alarm goes off, he starts roaring, and she starts roaring because why the hell does she have to get up when he gets up when she needs her sleep and she's dead for the day if she doesn't get it and my God, what a way to get up anyway, with all that hollering, as if the alarm wasn't bad enough.

"Then he's shouting at me because how can I go to school looking like a bum and she's yelling at him that that's a hell of a way to send a kid to school by yelling at him and my sister is screaming that she can't *think* in his goddamn house and the dog is jumping all over the place because somebody, like me, forgot to take her out last night and my father is banging his fist on the table because I have no sense of RESPONSIBILITY for anybody or anything and how can I do that to the poor dog, though to tell the truth, he'd like to throw that poor dog down the incinerator.

"So," Rob grinned, "now I get up before anybody and they can yell their lungs out—which they're doing right this second—but not at *me*. Next thing

I got to figure is how I can work it out so I don't get home until they're all asleep. That's a lot harder, but there's got to be a way."

"I get it at night," Sam said, "but the morning's okay. My father, he's gone before I get up. My mother used to get on me at breakfast, like where's the work I was supposed to do last night or WHEN are you going to get a haircut and stop looking like a sheep dog. You know. But she's mostly given up because I learned how to fix that. When she starts in, I just don't say nothing. Nothing at all. Drives her crazy. Wears her out. Fast."

"That wouldn't work at my house," Rob said. "Nobody pays attention to each other, to whether they're reacting or not. They just yell. They wouldn't hear silence. They only hear themselves."

Saddlefield, the tall, thin blond boy whom Sam best remembered as being backed against a wall by a steaming Rob Holmes, passed them, glanced worriedly at Rob, and went to the far end of the gate where he started looking through a notebook while still taking quick looks at Rob. After a few minutes, Saddlefield put the notebook in his book bag and went down the street away from the school.

"One thing I can't figure out," Sam said, gesturing in Saddlefield's direction, "is why you're so down on him. I mean, just him. That other guy, he was the one who snatched your book in the first place."

"Yeah." Rob was still looking at Saddlefield in the distance. "But that other guy didn't drop it into the gutter. That's not it, though. There's something about that punk, Saddlefield, that I never did like anyway. And now, once he did that, ruining something I can never get again, I ought to really take care of him."

"But how? You told him you weren't going to beat him up, so how are you going to get him?"

Rob smiled, a peculiar mixture of cunning and sheepishness, and said: "I'm not going to do a damn thing to that squeaky bastard. I'm just going to let him keep on thinking that something awful—so awful that there's no way he can even imagine it—is going to happen to him at any second. I mean, if you can keep somebody terrified all the time, that's much worse than any beating. And it doesn't get you expelled. The only thing . . ."

"Yeah?"

"The only thing"—Rob screwed up his nose—"is that I don't know how long I can keep it up. I hate the creep, no question about that. But, I don't know, I don't seem to be able to hate very hard very long. And I'm beginning to feel a little funny whenever I see him, knowing he's so scared of me."

"Your problem," said Sam, "is that you're just not mean. You're beginning to feel a little sorry for him."

"Damn." Rob shook his head. "I *want* to keep it up, I do, but you may be right. Maybe I ought to get up later. If I go back to having breakfast with my family, that ought to make me mean enough."

XI

"You have to be in *court* tomorrow?" The headmaster stared at Sam.

"Yes, sir. I was using a subway pass that wasn't mine and that had expired anyway. You see, a friend of mine had lost his and he borrowed mine and then he lost mine and found his and gave it to me in place of mine, and well, since I am entitled to a subway pass, I don't think there was anything wrong in my using it. But a subway guard thought different."

"What will you plead?" the headmaster asked.

"Guilty. With an explanation. The one I just gave you."

"Explanations won't do you any good, but I'll give you an excuse for tomorrow morning's absence. You'll come right back here, of course. Breaking the law doesn't give you a holiday." Mr. Monk wrote out a note to himself. "Well, the school does have to cooperate with the criminal justice system although, I must say, we've not had any criminals at Burr for a long time."

"Will this go on my record?"

"Not on your record at Burr." The headmaster bit down on a smile. "The judge is not a member of the faculty. All I want to know, as an official of *this* institution, is whether you are now aware that you did something wrong."

"God," said Sam, sighing, "anything that causes this much trouble must be wrong, I guess. But I don't feel like a criminal, if that's what you mean."

"But you won't do it again because it's not worth all this trouble, right?"

"Right," Sam said.

"Then I suppose"—the headmaster rose, signaling the end of the interview—"that you have, as they say, learned your lesson. Though without contrition, which is too bad, but at least you won't repeat the offense. Do tell me what the judge said and by the way, I don't think you'll have to bring a toothbrush with you when you go down to the halls of justice."

"Sir," Sam said at the door, "this whole thing may seem funny to *you*, but I'm a little scared."

"That, my boy, is precisely what the law is for—to instill fear. The law works when the vast majority of citizens are so fearful of breaking its commandments that they prefer not to. It may often be the case, as Mr. Dickens said, that 'the law is a ass,' but that does not make the law any less of a pain in that part of the anatomy with the same nomenclature."

"My father quotes somebody, I don't know who: 'He that goes to law holds a wolf by the ear.' "

"Richard Burton," the headmaster said airily. *The Anatomy of Melancholy*. But in this instance, the wolf is holding *you* by the ear."

Sam sighed again. "I know."

"But it is such a busy wolf and you are such a minor offender that it won't hold you long. I am sure I shall see you tomorrow—without shackles. But if not, we shall send you your assignments during your confinement. Learning must go on, against all odds."

That night, in his dreams, Sam was being relentlessly pursued by a red-eyed wolf riding a snickering ass. The wolf had the face of Transit Officer Felipe Cruz, who kept snarling: "This boy steals rides! What do you do with a boy that steals rides? You put him where he can't move nowhere, right? R-i-i-i-ght! Hey, watch that schoolboy go! He's looking *good*! Good enough to eat."

The ass gave out a great guffaw and its face, Sam saw, was that of Mr. Levine-Griffin.

At quarter of nine the next morning, Sam, alone, stood before a huge, dreary building of gray marble.

In long, bleak, carved letters over the revolving doors, an inscription advised:

EVERY PLACE IS SAFE TO HIM
WHO LIVES IN JUSTICE.
BE JUST AND FEAR NOT.

Walking up the stairs, Sam did not feel safe. Looking at the ticket that Officer Cruz had given him, Sam took the elevator and got off at the eleventh floor. The narrow, gloomy room where he and Justice were to meet was already full of offenders—mostly shabby adults whom Sam half expected to ask him if he had any spare change. But there were also some fallen scholars like himself, and all but a few had a parent with them. Sam rather wished he had, too.

"All rise!" A beefy, white-haired man in a uniform bellowed the command from the front of the room as a tall, spare man with bald head, glasses, and black robe took his seat behind a long raised desk. The judge seemed no more pleased to be in this room than everyone else in it.

Being in the last row, for there was no other place to sit, Sam found it hard to make out what was happening. The defendants mumbled, and the judge mostly listened, skeptically. When he did speak, his voice appeared to be under water. No case took longer than a few minutes, although occasionally, when a youngster was involved, a parent would try to launch into a most earnest, intimate appeal to the judge's impassive, flinty face. These speeches the judge would abruptly cut off, grumble something to the court clerk below him, and look gloomily up at the ceiling until the clerk called the next name. Which suddenly was:

"Sam Davidson!"

Pulling on his ear, looking down at his shoes, and wondering how on earth he had put on a pair that didn't match, Sam walked stiffly to the front of the room and stopped, gazing up at the judge who was reading a sheet of paper.

"Trying to use a subway pass that was not yours, and if it had been yours was no good anyway," the judge said in a soft growl as he peered at Sam. And then looked again at the paper before him. "Burr Academy. That used to be quite a school. Hard to get in. Made a big thing of building character. Guess it's gone downhill like everything else. Takes in boys who try to sneak through turnstiles."

"Sir, that's not fair!" Sam said in a louder voice than he had intended. "I wasn't sneaking. And I've never been in trouble before. And you can't blame the school for what I did, anyway. I always thought a judge is supposed to be very careful about things like that."

The clerk, coughing hard to suppress a laugh, turned his back to the bench for a moment. The judge, his eyebrows lifting, leaned forward and looked closely at Sam, who had started to paw the ground a little. "My, my," he said gruffly, "we have a young man here who thinks it his responsibility to judge the judge."

Sam had a great urge, which he managed to control, to bang himself on the head. "All I meant," he said, "was that the other kids at Burr shouldn't be lumped in with me."

"Oh"—the judge tapped a pencil on the desk—"you're the only bad apple." Suddenly he shook his head in exasperation. "That's not quite what I meant to say—since you are still presumed innocent. You ought to learn to watch your tongue, young man, and then you wouldn't provoke people to say more than they really intended to say."

"I didn't start it," Sam mumbled.

The court clerk once again was seized with a desperate need to cough, and the judge glared at him. "If it's all right with you, young man," the tall man in the black robe said dryly, "we shall proceed. How do you plead—guilty or not guilty?"

"Guilty, sir, with an explanation," and Sam told the judge the history of the shared bus pass.

Scratching his nose, the judge said: "Do you realize that you have implicated your friend—what's his name, Benjy Bloom—in this course of unlawful conduct? According to your story, *he* used *your* subway pass, to which he was not entitled, before he managed to lose it."

Sam closed his eyes, groaned, and looked up at the judge. "I wasn't thinking, Your Honor. That was a terrible thing of me to say. He's not a criminal, sir. Can we just stay with my case? I mean, can he be left out of it?"

"You'll inform him of the consequences of his ever using a fraudulent pass again?"

"Oh yes, sir. I'll be like an example to him, Your Honor."

"Hmmph. If that's what you have in mind, then I ought to impose a severe penalty on you, wouldn't you say? Otherwise, what kind of an example would you be?"

"But I didn't *mean* to do anything wrong," Sam howled as softly as he could. "I just wasn't thinking."

"I do not understand"—the judge appeared to be talking to the clock on the wall at the back of the room—"why young people these days have stopped thinking of consequences. I do not understand why they gratify their instincts, like the very animals in the field. And then, afterward, when they are brought to justice, they haven't the slightest remorse. Just explanations. They are full of *explanations*." He practically spit out the last word.

Sam wondered if he'd get out of jail by the time he was twenty-one.

"However"—the judge stared at Sam again, not too unkindly—"the total precipitous decline of this society is not the business of this court. We deal with just one rip in the fabric at a time. And in your case, young man, this being a first offense, and this proceeding having filled you with apprehension, if not remorse, I will adjourn your case in contemplation of dismissal."

"Huh?" said Sam.

" 'Huh, *Your Honor*.' Or 'huh, *sir*.' Your case will be dismissed in six months provided you do not get into any trouble with the law before then. And dismissal will mean that there will be no permanent record of your wrongdoing."

"Thank you," said Sam. "Sir."

"Woe unto you, young man"—the judge picked up another folder—"if I see you in the next six months. Or thereafter. For God's sake, boy"—he tried a wintry smile—"learn to *think* before you act. It'll save you being burdened by explanations all your life for what you've done. That way, you'll be able to walk straight. Look around you. Most people don't."

As the court officer intoned the name of the next case, Sam, with a large grin, bolted out of the courtroom, found a phone booth, called home, and yelled, "Mom, I'm free! I beat the rap!"

XII

The second side of the tape was full, and as Sam pulled a fresh cassette out of his pocket, Major Kelley, stretching, said: "Take five. How about a Coke?"

As Sam nodded, the musician walked into the kitchen which, Sam saw, was just as spotlessly well-ordered as the spacious combination living room-bedroom in which he was seated. It was the first floor of a brownstone on the far west of Greenwich Village, near the Hudson River, and Kelley had lived there for more than thirty years.

Neatly arrayed all along one wall were brass plaques, engraved citations, scrolls—like diplomas and certificates of achievement in a doctor's office—that had been awarded to Kelley through the decades. Some commemorated his having won *Down Beat* readers' polls in the early forties, but others—from Japan, France, Sweden, England, and Argentina—were more recent.

"They remember you longer overseas," Kelley said when he returned with the Coke and noticed

Sam examining the wall of trophies. "They take jazz more seriously, because it's not theirs. Just like Americans take Beethoven and Bach more seriously, because they're not ours. And also, because they're not black. Very hard for you people to consider *anything* black as real serious culture, you know."

"I do," Sam said quickly. "I take jazz real seriously."

"Well, you're learning. But most American kids don't get a chance to learn about this country's own classical music. Boy, how many of your schoolmates know anything about King Oliver, Bessie Smith, Lester Young, Charlie Parker, John Coltrane? Even Duke Ellington? How many have heard, even once, Duke's 'Reminiscing in Tempo,' 'Black Beauty,' 'Black, Brown and Beige'? I ask you, how many? Have *you*?"

Acutely embarrassed, Sam shook his head from side to side.

"Of course not." Kelley pulled on his mustache. "Where *would* you hear them? Not in school. Not on the radio, except some oddball FM stations at oddball times. And certainly not on television. It's a damn shame, boy, letting kids grow up so ignorant of their own country's culture. Hell, it's downright unpatriotic. Now you go to a high-class school, probably the best in the city. And I am willing to bet you five thousand dollars that there's not *one* little course on jazz. It's like all of us who have ever been in this music are invisible.

"Well"—Kelley stood up and looked out the window—"there's nothing I can do about it. I could go live in some other country, like friends of mine have done, but that'd make me grow old too fast. That's what happens when you're cut off from your roots. I tried it, you know, years ago. Lived in Paris, and then in Amsterdam, but people there, they're good people, but they move different, the rhythms of their talk are different, the streets aren't my streets, they got no old memories for me. Even the booze is different. I mean, you may get the same brand you take here, but somehow it tastes different there. The air is different. The light in the air is different. And so are the night sounds. Those places aren't real to me, boy. So I got no choice but here. I ought to be glad, I guess, that at my age, I still got the chops to play and that I still get gigs. But, when I let myself think about it, it does hurt me that most people in this country haven't the slightest idea I'm even here, that any of us have been here. Ever heard Edmond Hall, boy?"

Sam had not.

"Clarinet player with a sound that went right through your soul. And a beat! My God, he could make you jump sitting down. A gentleman, too, a real gentleman. A student of the music who was always helping young players. And he died. Hardly anybody but us musicians paid any mind. Hardly anybody but us musicians calls his name now. Just another jazzer that the Butcher cut down."

Kelley was silent for a while, looking at his hands. Abruptly, he rose. "Come," he said to Sam. "I want you to meet somebody."

They went up the stairs, to the very top of the building, the fourth floor, where Kelley stopped at a gleaming black door, took hold of a smartly polished brass knocker, and rapped it sharply against the door.

The door opened just a crack, and then wider. Peering out was an old man, with just about enough flesh to cover his skeleton. Stooped, not a hair on his head, he was wearing a white shirt, black tie, and a pair of dark brown pants that Sam saw went with the suit jacket neatly draped on a kitchen chair in a direct line of vision from the door.

The old man looked so fragile that, as Kelley introduced them, Sam barely touched his hand, afraid that any pressure at all might do some harm. But before he could take his hand away, it was seized in a clawlike grip that was so strong it made Sam wince.

"My father," said Major Kelley. "Alexander Dumas Kelley. And this," the musician said to the old man, "is Sam. Sam Davidson. He's writing a story about me."

Alexander Dumas Kelley looked quizzically at Sam, waved them inside the apartment, closed the door, locked it, and motioned them into the small kitchen. The only other room, somewhat larger, had a bed, a chair, and books. Three walls jammed with books, from floor to ceiling, and more books stacked carefully in high piles on the floor.

"We don't live together," the old man said to Sam in a high but surprisingly firm voice, "because we get on each other's nerves. Always have. It's not that we don't like and respect each other, you understand, but we're both stubborn. Stubborn as hell. And fortunately, I don't have to live with him. Or anybody. Got my pension from the Post Office. And my investment." The old man clapped his hands together as if he were applauding himself.

"When I was coming up in the world," the elder Kelley said, then stopped. "Don't usually have visitors, that's why I'm talking so much, but it could do you some good. Anyway, like I was saying, when I was a boy, selling newspapers, I'd see all the lights go on at night. Everywhere. So did everybody else, of course, but I decided those lights were going to be my security, and just about everything I saved, I put into electricity company stock. They didn't care if I was black or green or purple with yellow spots. All they wanted to know was if my money was good.

"So, for a long, long time, every night, before I'd go to bed, I'd stand by the window and look out to check how my investment was doing. Every time somebody put on a light, there was something in it for me. But then, I saw a *better* investment: IBM. The folks there were looking way ahead in what they were doing. So I put all my electricity company stock in IBM. So now, old as I am, I ain't dependent on *nobody*. I still miss the feeling those lights at night gave me, though. Anyway, this boy"—the old man looked at Major—"he never does think ahead. Never did. That's why I didn't want him to go grow up to be a musician. They're all like that. They only live for today."

Major Kelley laughed. "Hell, old man. I haven't asked you for a nickel for fifty years. I split out of his place"—the musician turned to Sam—"when I was just about your age. Wasn't nobody going to tell me what I was going to do."

"Nobody could, that's true," the old man smiled. "Way too late to change any of that anyway. That's why we get along now. Neither of us tells the other what to do. Although," the old man chuckled, "I'm waiting till he's so broke, he's gonna have to move in with me."

"I'll set up in a doorway first, old man," said Major Kelley. "But it won't come to that. Something always turns up."

Through the open door into the bedroom, Sam

was trying to read some of the titles of the vast array of books.

"All history," said the old man, watching him. "Histories of my people. Late at night, I go into other centuries and listen to amazing people. Amazing black people. Survivors, every one. The others, they thought my people were animals. Worse than animals. Nobody ever beat an animal the way some of my people were beaten. But those others, *they* were the ignorant ones. Nothing dumber than a dumb white man. No offense, boy. All of you weren't that bad, but a powerful lot of you were. Still are."

"Okay, old man," said Major Kelley, "I didn't bring this child up for a whipping."

"Aw"—his father waved Kelley away—"this child knows it's not personal."

Sam nodded, somewhat doubtfully.

"About these books"—the old man beamed at his library—"they're here to keep me company and they're here because I sure do admire survivors. Him, for instance." He pointed to Major Kelley. "The one thing I say about this child of mine is that he keeps on keeping on. He's never been a whiner. He takes that fool horn of his—him that could have been a doctor or something big—and he makes his own way. I give him that."

"They know your son all over the world," Sam volunteered.

71

The old man wrinkled his nose. "Some do. But most don't. But nobody knows me at all, so I guess he's gone beyond his father."

"Even without stock in IBM," said Major Kelley with a grin.

"Day's gonna come when you'll wish you had some of that stock," said his father. "But then, I guess you will have it. When I die. If I die. I'm not fixing to die, boy," the old man said to Sam.

"No, sir," Sam felt called upon to say.

"Well, you come back when you want to," the old man leaned toward Sam. " I might even let you borrow one of the books."

"Thank you, sir."

"I might. Once I find out if you're a serious boy or not."

Major Kelley got up, followed by Sam, and the old man, seeing them to the door, put a long, bony finger on Sam's shoulder. "Tell me, how come you're writing a story about my son?" the elder Kelley asked.

"It's for school."

"Imagine that. They're studying Major here in a school? And he never *finished* any school. Ain't that something?"

"There's different kinds of schools, old man," said his son.

"I know, I know," the old man smiled. "The school of hard knocks, and what not. But I still say you would have made one hell of a doctor—and saved me a lot of money in my gathering infirmities."

Major Kelley roared with laughter. "If I was a doctor, you never would do *one* thing I told you to."

"Not so you'd know it," his father said, much amused. "But when I was alone, maybe I would."

On the way downstairs, Major Kelley said to Sam: "I figure that since you're going to write about me, you might as well see my roots. That's some marvelous old ornery man, isn't he?"

Sam nodded vigorously.

"He's my model, you know," the musician said. "Damned if I'd ever tell him that. But that man is a champion survivor. And, you know, I'm not so sure he *is* ever gonna die."

XIII

In the locker room Sam, Rob, and Abner Williams were arguing. Diagonally across from them, in a corner, Jeremiah Saddlefield, alone, watched the debate.

"No way." Abner was shaking his head. "No way a black's going to be President before the first woman President. White woman, of course. And no black's going to be President for a long time after that, either."

"Come on," said Rob. "A *woman* commander in chief of the armed forces? I'm no sexist, you know, but the country wouldn't go for that."

"England got its first woman prime minister," Sam said. "She gives the orders to the generals."

"Sure," Rob grinned. "But only after England stopped being any kind of world power. It depends on *us* now for protection, and I bet you any woman prime minister there wouldn't want a woman President here."

"Why?" Sam was hunting for his shoes. "What's

74

the difference? A woman can push a button just as well as a man, and that's what the next war is going to be all about. All two and a half minutes of it."

"Well, you know," Rob said, neatly kicking one of Sam's shoes under his own locker, "women aren't as steady as men. They get more excited. And there goes the planet!"

"But you're not sexist, right?" Sam laughed. "I know guys who blow up if you just *look* at them. You're not making any sense. But you're probably right about a woman President. A lot of people still think the way you do, so I guess there'll be a black *male* President before any woman."

"You are *both* out of your skulls." Abner pounded his large thigh for emphasis. "This country would elect a horse before they'd have a black President. Hell, right now, you see one of us being president of one of the TV networks or an oil company or General Motors? Then how is one of us going to get to be president of *everything*? I mean, look it up, look around, this is one racist country."

"It's getting better," said Rob. "Long way to go, but it's getting better."

"Yeah?" Abner pointed a black finger at him. "How many whites you know who, deep down, all the way down, are *not* prejudiced? Think about it hard. Go down the list of your parents and your relatives and anybody else you know. And *then* tell me about a black being President of the United States. You know something? If it was a horse that got elected, it'd be a white horse."

Sam started to sniff, and then looked toward Saddlefield who, in his corner, was inhaling, with great concentration, from what seemed to be a very ragged remnant of a cigarette.

"Jees," Sam shouted, "what an idiot!" Then, his voice much lower, he said to Saddlefield, "Everybody knows they catch you with dope, you get thrown out!"

Abner sniffed the air, too, and left immediately. Only Sam, Rob, and Saddlefield were left in the locker room.

"Stupid," Sam said to Saddlefield through his teeth, "get *rid* of it!"

"No," Rob snapped, "you're so cool, Saddlefield, why don't you stick it in your ear and go into class with it? Just like the world-champion moron you are!"

Saddlefield's face grew tight. Biting his lips, glaring at Rob, he flipped what he had in his hand in Rob's direction. Then, reaching into his shoe, took out two more of the cigarettes and threw those too as he ran out of the locker room.

Rob stood looking at them on the ground in front of him. Sam, who was nearer the bathroom, said: "Give them to me. I'll flush them down the toilet." As Rob was passing him the cigarettes, they heard a sniff like a rhinoceros's and saw, coming into the locker room from the back entrance, Mr. Levine-Griffin.

"I will take those," he said coldly as he slipped an envelope out of his breast pocket, removed the letter inside, and held the empty envelope out to Rob who put the three cigarettes into it.

"It wasn't ours!" Sam shouted indignantly as he saw a ruddy glow of triumph spread over Levine-Griffin's usually milk-white face.

"Really?" Levine-Griffin said in total, complacent disbelief as he kneeled down and checked the floor for any more evidence. Not finding any, but patting his breast pocket where he had returned the envelope with its new contents, Levine-Griffin looked contemptuously at Sam. "Really? This illegal substance, this marijuana, snuck up on you, did it? It just leaped into your hands?"

Sam and Rob both looked as if they'd been kicked in the stomach. "We got to tell him," said Sam. "It's not ratting when that creep practically set us up." Rob nodded, but rubbed his forehead hard.

"Sir," said Sam, "that stuff was Saddlefield's. We saw him smoking one just before the bell. I told him to get rid of it and he threw it over here, and then two more, and he ran. That's exactly what happened."

Levine-Griffin was no longer smiling. His flush

now was of anger—bright, rising anger. "It would be disgusting and cowardly enough for you, both of you, to try to escape your just punishment by falsely accusing another student. But to deliberately pick out a boy who is already suffering painfully in this school because of his inability to make friends is so cruel, so mean-spirited, that if I could, I would have you each expelled thrice. Once, for possession of an absolutely prohibited drug. Once, for bearing vicious false witness against another student. And once, for persecuting this particular poor, lonely child."

"Poor, lonely child!" Rob couldn't restrain himself. "Saddlefield is a whiny, sneaky pain in the ass. Why do you think nobody in the school can stand him? Because he has all the personality of a cockroach."

"And so"—Levine-Griffin had taken the envelope out of his pocket again as if to reassure himself that the evidence had not somehow been spirited out of his possession—"and so, having decided that this boy is a pariah to be stepped upon like a cockroach —your very word—you saw nothing wrong with his being blamed and punished for that which he did not do."

"No!" Sam howled. "We told you exactly what happened. That's *his* stuff, not *ours!*"

"Well," said Levine-Griffin, "I suppose that once one has taken the path you two have chosen, there is no lie, no act of dishonor, no betrayal, no self-debasement of which one is not capable. All right, Holmes, Davidson, you are coming with me to see the headmaster."

"I got a right to a phone call," said Sam.

"No, you don't. I am not putting you under arrest. The way you're going, you are likely to have that experience one day, but this is not the day. This is school discipline day. This is the day of the ultimate school discipline. As soon as you are expelled, you may call mommy. Or daddy. Although I think Mr. Monk will do that first."

"Good God," Rob said to Sam, "that little bastard has fixed us for life."

"The hell he has." Sam stared ahead. "After all the trouble I was in where I came from, I'll be damned if I'll be kicked out of here for something I didn't do. No matter how bad it looks right now, the truth's got to count for something."

"Truth? Truth?" Levine-Griffin snickered exaggeratedly. "That word coming from you is a nullity, a void. Worse, it is a veritable Black Mass, a mockery of everything that glorious word, *truth,* means to those who can look at themselves in the mirror without casting down their eyes."

Sam dug his fingers into his scalp. "Sir, you've said in class that what makes this country different from most others is that here the accused is always presumed innocent until *proved* guilty."

"Out there"—Levine-Griffin waved toward the

whole nation outside the window—"yes. But *here,* in this school, in this private school, we are not bound by so time-consuming a principle if we catch someone in flagrante delicto. As has just happened, with the contraband passing from one corrupt young man to another. Presumed *innocent?* How can that be when I—with my very own eyes—have come upon you immersed in your guilt? Reeking of your guilt!"

"Sir"—Sam looked up at Levine-Griffin and asked—"does this school have capital punishment?"

"Are you so hardened, young man, that you can joke at this moment when your future is in ruins?"

"Just wanted to make sure," said Sam. "The way you've been talking, I wanted to know if you're taking us to be shot. With the trial after, you know, like in those countries without human rights."

"Get moving!" Levine-Griffin moved as if to shove Sam, and then stayed his hand. "Let's see how much of a comedian you are when you see the headmaster."

XIV

The headmaster had not said a word. First, Levine-Griffin had presented the case for the prosecution, holding the envelope at arm's length as if it were dangerously infectious. And every time he mentioned either Sam's or Rob's name, which was clangingly often, the head of the high school pointed the envelope at their respective satanic hearts.

"Therefore," Levine-Griffin had concluded, looking for a place to bang his fist and smiting the air for lack of a solid surface, "for the health and integrity of Burr Academy, and of every student in it, these two must be expelled. Immediately. I do not use 'health' as a metaphor. There is no telling how many innocents these two will infect if they are allowed to remain. They are cancers and must be removed, root and branch."

Mr. Monk, his face expressionless, nodded to Sam and Rob to begin. With Rob mainly providing a heated obbligato of "Yeah!" "That's *exactly* what happened," "Right! Right!" and other indignant exclamations, Sam was the main spokesman for the defense. His face red, his voice cracking with anger and fear, Sam, by a mighty effort of will, stuck to the facts and refrained from adding any violent adjectives to Saddlefield's name. Every time he did pronounce that name, however, it was as if he were referring to a stopped-up toilet.

"That's it," Sam had finished. "That's the whole truth. I can see how it looked to Mr. Levine-Griffin when he walked in and just me and Rob were there. And the stuff. But he wouldn't listen to us. He made up his mind as soon as he came in. It was as if we had long criminal records. As if we had done such awful things here, so many awful things, and told so many lies, that there was no way we *could* be believed. But that's not true. You know that's not true." Sam looked straight at the headmaster.

"*I* know what *I* saw," Levine-Griffin bellowed. "All of this is just a smokescreen."

Mr. Monk looked intently at the boys, and then said to Levine-Griffin, "I want to see Saddlefield before his first class tomorrow."

"Aw," Rob roared in disgust, then roaring all the more because Sam's elbow had dug into his ribs, "that creep will just lie."

"See," said Levine-Griffin, "they fear the truth from the lad they have tried so foully to besmirch."

"You have made a grave accusation against Saddlefield," the headmaster said to Rob. "Possession of a drug that automatically leads to expulsion. Are you suggesting I simply take your word for it and expel *him?*"

Rob bit his lip. "No, he's got a right to be heard. And," he added bitterly, "to lie."

"So how will I know who's telling the truth?" the headmaster asked.

"Isn't that why you're the headmaster?" Sam said. "Because you've got the judgment, the experience, or whatever, to tell the difference between those of us who are liars and those of us who aren't?"

"But what if there is no other evidence," Monk said, "than the marijuana in the envelope Mr. Levine-Griffin has in his hand? Evidence that points only at you."

"But that *isn't* the only evidence." Sam was practically running in place in his agitation. "*We're* the evidence, too, Rob and me. And Saddlefield. It's when you put us all together in your mind—when you examine who each of us *is*—that you'll know who's telling the truth."

"Imagine if we ran our courts that way," Levine-Griffin said scornfully. "Each judge would decide a case on how he *felt* about a defendant. Nonsense. Absolute nonsense."

"You said"—Rob, breathing hard, turned to Levine-Griffin—"that Burr is different from the way it is outside, the way it is in the rest of the country.

You said there is no presumption of innocence at Burr. So why are you bringing in the way the courts work?"

"Is that what you said?" the headmaster, frowning, asked the head of the high school. "No presumption of innocence at Burr?"

"I said"—Levine-Griffin glared at Rob—"that when someone is caught red-handed in a private school which runs its own affairs, which has its own methods of governance, there is no presumption of innocence. But actually, this applies anywhere. If a policeman sees a man with a gun in the process of holding someone up, the presumption of innocence is fiction."

"Still," said the headmaster, "your man with a gun would get a hearing and a trial. Look, obviously the evidence against these two is very damaging, extremely damaging. But we're not finished yet. After I talk with Saddlefield"—he looked at Sam and Rob —"I shall see you two again. And your parents."

"They will, of course, not be attending classes," said Levine-Griffin.

"I can't punish them until I convict them, can I?" the headmaster answered. "That's even more elementary than the presumption of innocence. I'm not going to drag this out, but until I do come to a decision, they will go about their regular business."

"But they'll infect the school," Levine-Griffin almost wailed.

"If they are drug users," said Monk, "I can't imagine they'd be so stupid as to carry the stuff around while they're under investigation. So there's no immediate danger of their infecting the rest of the student body."

"As if some kids even in the middle school, let alone the high school, haven't already found dope by themselves," Rob snorted and then yelped at Sam's foot banging into his ankle.

"That's probably true," the headmaster said icily to Rob. So icily that Rob dropped his eyes and watched himself rub his ankle. "It's a very, very difficult problem keeping drugs out of this school. And from what I hear, out of just about any school. But I very much resent the casualness of your attitude about it. If some of the children in the middle school *are* smoking marijuana, or swallowing pills, I don't find that at all amusing. Our responsibility here is to develop clear minds, not muddled ones. Above all, we want everyone who graduates to know how to solve problems with his or her head, not to cover them over with some weed or chemical."

"I'm sorry," Rob said. "I just got mad at the idea that we could be some kind of danger to everybody, that we're addicts and pushers, you know."

"Ho-de-ho-ho," said Levine-Griffin, "behold these angels, come from on high to light up our lives."

The headmaster stood up. "As I said, I intend this to come to a swift conclusion. Now"—he turned to

Sam and Rob—"if, before I call you in again, you have something to tell me, just come right in. You won't need an appointment."

"Come in to confess, you mean," said Sam.

"If that is what I had wanted to say," the headmaster said coolly, "that is what I would have said."

"Oh, they'll never confess." Levine-Griffin had folded his hands over his stomach and was contemplating the accused. "If I have ever seen boys without remorse . . ."

"Well," Sam said, "I'm a little sorry about that bank job we pulled a couple of weeks ago. The teller got fired for giving all that money to just a couple of kids."

"Davidson!" The headmaster's voice was like a whip.

"Yes, sir?"

"Not funny. Not in the least funny, and most inopportune. I don't think you have any real idea of how much trouble you're in. I believe, I absolutely believe, that Mr. Levine-Griffin saw what he says he saw. I also believe that you are a hairsbreadth away from being expelled from this school. Now do you understand me?"

"Yes, sir," said Sam, looking down. "You're right. It's not funny."

XV

Saddlefield saw them coming after him in the corridor, but he didn't run. Leaning against the wall, indeed shrinking against the wall, he said—as Sam and Rob stopped on either side of him—"No."

"You're gonna let us get thrown out because of what *you* did?" Sam's hands were jammed into his pockets as he spoke because he knew he couldn't trust them if they were free.

"I didn't plan it that way," Saddlefield said very softly. "I really didn't. I didn't plan anything. It all just happened. But the only alternative to you guys getting thrown out is me getting thrown out. My father would kill me. I don't mean physically. He'd act as if I was dead—forever. My father is a very hard man. Maybe the hardest man there is. So you see, I got no choice. I'm sorry, I'm truly sorry, not that that means anything to you. But I got no choice."

"You just confessed," said Sam.

Saddlefield shook his head. "You guys really think I'm stupid. I never said a thing. Whatever you say I said, I never said a thing."

"We got it on tape." Rob patted his pants pocket as Sam's eyes widened.

"You just thought of that this second," Saddlefield said, looking at that pocket which had no bulge in it. No bulge at all. "But thanks for warning me. I got nothing more to say to you guys—ever. But I am sorry."

"That does it!" Rob's hands moved toward Saddlefield's throat.

"Go ahead," Saddlefield said. "You think a beating means anything compared to getting expelled? Anyway, if you even touch me, I'll tell the headmaster you were trying to beat a phony confession out of me."

Sam grabbed Rob's arm. "Not yet," he said. "After we clear ourselves, we'll take care of this turd. But not yet."

Saddlefield looked at his watch and then at the boys. "I assume I can leave?"

They turned and walked away. Rob clenched his fists and walked faster and faster, Sam trotting along beside him. "Damn," Rob said, looking around and seeing that Saddlefield had disappeared. "If only I *had* a tape recorder on me."

"Well, that's out now." Sam rubbed his nose.

"That bastard will never break. He's too slippery to break."

They stopped outside the library, stared at each other and then out the window and then at the walls and the bulletin boards and then out the window again.

"Try the ceiling," said the tall, red-haired girl standing just inside the door of the library. "Maybe what you're looking for is up there. Or maybe I can help."

"Nobody can help," Sam mumbled. "But thanks, Rebecca. It's just nothing we can talk about."

"Oh, I know all about it," she said. "I heard Levine-Griffin telling about his great detective work and about what shameless liars you guys are. It was in the faculty lounge. You would have thought he was on TV or something. You could hear him from the corridor. Wow, you two are in some mess."

"He's got it all wrong, you know," Rob said.

"Of course, I know," Rebecca shook her long hair in irritation. "What do you take me for? Even if you guys weren't such goody-goodies, which you really are underneath all that huffing and puffing, you're too smart to have any dope on you in school. Well, that rotten Saddlefield isn't going to tell the truth, and the only witness, God help us, is Levine-Griffin. What are you going to *do*?"

"There's only one thing *to* do," said Rob. "We got to make Saddlefield talk."

"Unless"—Sam was frowning—"unless the headmaster is able to see through it all, even without Saddlefield telling what really happened."

"What are you going to ask Santa Claus for this year?" Rob snapped.

"Rob's right," said Rebecca. "Why would the headmaster go against Levine-Griffin, who was *there*, for God's sake? No, we've got to nail that reject, Saddlefield."

"Hey," Sam grinned, "you said 'we.' "

"Damn straight," Rebecca smoothed her hair. "This school is boring enough without you two getting kicked out. Then it would be absolutely dismal. Nobody running people down, like a truck, in the corridors. Nobody picking up their book bags upside down. Nobody blowing up like a volcano in class. Nobody behaving like two cute bulls in this stuffy china shop."

"Cute!" Rob grimaced.

"Never mind," Sam said. "I'll accept that. Coming from where it does, I mean."

"Oh-h-h," Rob smiled. "Well, what do you know?"

"You don't know a damn thing," Rebecca, turning to Rob, said sharply. "It's just like you. Instead of concentrating on saving your neck, you're making silly assumptions about something that isn't any of your business anyway. Now, we've got to have a plan. Tonight, each of us has really got to do some thinking. And we'll meet in front of the school at seven tomorrow. Seems to me that the three of us can outsmart that one sneak, right?"

Sam and Rob nodded, but not very vigorously.

XVI

For once, neither his father nor his mother interrupted as Sam told the whole story—from the locker room to the headmaster's office. His mother lit a cigarette, then another while the first was still alive in the ashtray. His father kept tapping the eraser end of a pencil on the table, his eyes never leaving his son's face.

"That's it," Sam ended. "So far."

"You have any doubt that we believe you?" his father said.

"I'd like to hear what you believe." Sam looked at him solemnly.

His father leaned across the table and mussed up Sam's hair. "Like you told Monk, *you're* the evidence, too. And you are not a liar. That's a marvelous thing to know about a child of yours—that he'll never lie to you. And I've *always* known that about you."

"Then why," his son said, "do you get so angry sometimes when I tell you the truth? Like when I got picked up for using Benjy's bus pass?"

"That's different." Sam's mother poured herself some more coffee. "When your child is so careless that he puts himself into a situation where he can harm himself, you get angry. Like when you were little and planted yourself in front of a truck on the street and wouldn't move. Couldn't tie your own shoelaces but you were going to face down that truck! And we whacked you good, or dad did. But that's *protective* anger. On the other hand, if we didn't know whether we could ever believe you, that would be so much worse than being angry. God, there'd be a knot in my stomach all the time. You see the difference?"

"I guess so," Sam said.

"And about this," his mother continued, "of course what you say happened *happened*."

Sam's father was pacing the kitchen. "It's weird," he said. "Being in this position with *another* head-master. When you think of the parents *I've* left in suspense. Damn it"—he looked at his wife—"my instinct is to call Monk right now."

"DO IT!" his wife slapped the table.

"But"—Carl Davidson stopped his pacing—"I know that I don't pay that much attention to calls I get from parents at a time like this. *Of course* they're going to say their kid is incapable of whatever disgraceful thing he's accused of doing Still . . ."

"CALL HIM!" his wife shouted.

Sam's father walked to the back room he used as a study and closed the door. On the phone, Richard Monk was sympathetic—as if, Carl Davidson thought, he was speaking to the bereaved at a funeral parlor.

"That's been my impression of Sam, too," Monk said. "A straight shooter, as we used to say. But if he is telling the truth, then Saddlefield faces expulsion. You know, I'll go a long way with a kid, give him every chance to redeem himself. Even when it comes to cheating. But I draw a very stiff line with drugs. I haven't cleaned them out of my school any more completely than I expect you, or any other headmaster or principal, has. But if there weren't the absolute certainty of expulsion for kids caught using and selling that poison, things would be much, much worse at Burr."

"That's my policy too at Alcott," Sam's father said. "But the issue here is not school policy but who's telling the truth."

"And the problem, as I'm sure you're aware," Monk went on, "is that I need more than Sam's testimony, and Rob's, that *they* are telling the truth. Especially since the head of my high school is a very determined witness against them. Look, I know how difficult this is for you and your wife—"

"And Sam."

"Yes. And certainly Sam. I am going to try to

get to the bottom of this as quickly as I can. I'm seeing Saddlefield at eight in the morning and then I'll check out what he says with Sam and Rob Holmes."

"But what if you're no farther along then than you are now?" Carl Davidson asked.

There was a pause. "At some point, and soon, I am going to have to make a decision—with as much information as I have to go on. You've been through this. It's not pleasant."

"Remember Oliver Cromwell," said Sam's father.

"Oh," said Monk, "you know that one too. I guess everybody in our line of work should. I will indeed beseech myself, in the bowels of Christ, to consider the possibility that I may be mistaken. Whatever I do. But I must do *something*. Well, I am glad you called, because it would have been very hard for you not to call."

"Thanks," Carl Davidson said. "One thing I want to leave with you. The boy does not lie. He just doesn't. He can't."

"Tell me," said Monk, "if you were in my place right now and you heard a parent say that to you—"

"There is a difference between what you and I often hear—all kinds of extenuating circumstances, from broken families to bad companions—and the absolute statement I just made. If a parent told me his child never lied, that would weigh heavily on me. If I thought the parent was truthful."

"Oh my," Monk sighed. "Now you're insisting on joining your son in the dock in my court?"

"If that's necessary, yes. And it may be."

Immaculate as always, Major Kelley was wearing a crisp white shirt, a black bow tie, a black vest without any pockets, and—also without pockets—a freshly pressed pair of dark gray pants.

Kelley waved Sam to a seat in the living room. "Phone rings"—Kelley surveyed himself with satisfaction—"and I'm ready. The trumpet player never showed up at the Hotel Carlyle? I don't have to waste no time changing. Just put on the right jacket, and I can make the gig in-stant-ly. Phone rings. President of the United States is having a reception for the President of France, and the French cat lets out that he's been collecting my records for years and years. So, the President of the United States says to me on the phone, can you *please* get down here right away? Why, sure. Out the door I go.

"And if the phone doesn't ring?" Kelley sat down, straight, in a chair. "Well, I still look right to myself. If I am my only company for the evening, why should I spend the evening with someone who looks like a bum? What kind of respect is that from me to me? That's something you don't understand yet, boy. I see how you dress. You're a good old traditional boy—a slob. What you have not learned—and some people never do learn—is that you *feel* different when you're dressed right. You feel you can do more, be more, think faster. And so you can. But if you dress sloppy, you think sloppy—whether you're out there in the world, or all by yourself."

"I like to be comfortable." Sam slumped against the back of an easy chair.

"No, you like to be lazy. All your life you're going to be picking clothes off the rack. The only tailor you're going to know is some old cat in the corner of some dry cleaning store who'll be sewing on your cheap buttons that your wife won't do because that ain't woman's work anymore. It's a shame, the way you're going to look all your life, but if somebody just doesn't care about how he presents himself to the world, nothing more need be said."

Sam looked at his sneakers; his white socks (except that one was really gray); his crumpled tan slacks with large, ugly black and red spots from when he had put two uncapped felt-tip pens in his pocket; and his blue corduroy shirt, which looked as if it had often been used to carry potatoes in. Sam sighed. "It doesn't matter how I look—if I'm going to be thrown out of school."

Kelley took a large, gleaming snifter glass, poured in cognac from a Courvoisier bottle, suddenly snapped his fingers, put the glass down, went to the refrigerator, brought out a Coke, filled another glass with it, and handed it to Sam.

"Yes," said Kelley, "that would be fully occupy-

97

ing your mind at the moment. Well, from what you told me on the phone, we have only one way to go. We got to get the truth out of—what's his name? Don't tell me. I'm very good on names. Have to be in my business. People who come to hear you more than once feel hurt if you don't remember their names. Let's see. Horse, saddle. Wheat, field. Saddlefield."

Sam nodded. "But he has every reason *not* to tell the truth."

"That," said Kelley, gazing admiringly at the cognac, "is what we have to find for that boy. A reason. A reason that will give him no choice but to tell the truth. Now, what do you know about his family?"

"His family?" Sam frowned. "All I know is his father's got a lot of money."

"From what?"

"Newspapers. He owns newspapers. Not in New York, but all over the rest of the country."

"Oh." Kelley grinned broadly. "*That* Saddlefield. Now I got something to go on. Yes, sir, I can see a way to your deliverance."

"I don't understand," Sam said.

"You read fairy tales when you were a tiny boy?"

"Yeah. I read a lot of them. I used to pretend to be in them."

"Okay," said Kelley. "When the magic happened —swords with special powers, words that could unlock huge doors—they didn't tell you exactly *how* it happened, did they? Takes all the spice out of the story. Like if they'd had a diagram showing how to make one of them swords or how a door was programmed to respond to certain combinations of vowels—it wouldn't be a fairy tale anymore. It'd be like something you could read in *Popular Mechanics*. So boy, you *are* in one of those stories now. I am your fairy godfather—absolutely no sexual reference intended, you understand. I'm not married anymore but anyone spends the night here, you can be sure it's a lady. Okay, you let your fearless fairy godfather get to work. And meanwhile, you keep me informed of what's going down."

"I'd sure like to know what you're going to do." Sam, mystified, looked up at Kelley.

"Faith!" Kelley roared. "You got to have faith! In all those stories you read as a child, everything worked out right in the end, right? The good folk were released to go on and dress right and prosper. The bad guys got what was coming to them, and more. Right? Right. And all the while you were reading, you had faith that when you got to the last page, you weren't going to be let down. Same thing here."

Sam rose and said, in a tentative way, that he was grateful.

"No need to thank me," said Kelley, "until I deliver. Which I will."

"You going to look the same when I see you next?" Sam said with a smile.

"I am never the same, even though I may look the same," Kelley growled, "so it doesn't matter. Anyway, this is a modern fairy tale, boy. These days, we fairy godfathers don't need to change shape to get into somebody's head."

XVII

The elder Saddlefield was short, wiry, and blunt. Not so much deliberately rude as impatient with anything that did not bear directly on what immediately interested him. People who worked for him, the headmaster had read, reported that Derek Saddlefield's idea of small talk was to ask them if their children read his newspaper in that particular city and if so, what they liked about it. And what they didn't like about it.

In Mr. Monk's office that gray morning, Derek Saddlefield had listened to his son tell the headmaster that he knew nothing about the marijuana in the locker room, and that Sam and Rob had lied about him both to save themselves and because they hated him. Jeremiah reminded the headmaster that Rob had nearly assaulted him on the opening day of school and added that since that day Rob had been continually threatening him. Sam, Jeremiah went on, was Rob's friend, and Sam too had always made it clear that he despised him.

"I don't know why they hate me so." Jeremiah, his eyes brimming with tears, looked at the headmaster. "I guess it's because I won't have anything to do with dope, and that makes me a goody-goody to them. They've turned the other kids against me, too. It's been a lonely semester, sir."

Richard Monk was tapping a finger on his desk, looking at the father more often than at the son. "Neither Davidson nor Holmes," the headmaster said, "has any record of drug use. Here or anywhere. Both, while sometimes boisterous, have never been known to lie. Actually, they seem to have a compulsion to tell the truth, even when it damages them."

"They're very clever, sir," Jeremiah said.

"It seems to me," his father broke in, "that we are wasting time on this character analysis. Those two were caught red-handed by the head of your high school. I am at a loss to understand—and that is something that rarely happens to me—why this case has not already been closed."

"If you will bear with me for a few more minutes," Monk said to the newspaper publisher, "I should like to speak to you alone." Jeremiah Saddlefield looked imploringly toward his father. "Why can't I hear?" the boy said, his voice cracking. "It has to do with me."

"The headmaster seems to want a bit more rope for his own hanging," the elder Saddlefield said dryly, "and I shall indulge him. If it turns out to be something you need to know, Jeremiah, I'll tell you afterwards."

Frowning, his shoulders hunched, the boy, after looking back a couple of times, left the room.

"What I am about to say," the headmaster began, "is difficult for me, speaking to a father, and will be difficult for a father to hear."

"You will find," Derek Saddlefield said glacially, "that nobody makes things difficult for me. It's quite the other way around."

"To begin with," the headmaster said slowly, "it is very hard for me to believe that Davidson and Holmes are not telling the truth."

"Finish the thought," Saddlefield snapped.

"All right. I doubt the credibility of your son."

"But you can't prove your doubt." Saddlefield's smile was more a snarl. "And you want me to tell you whether Jeremiah has a history of lying, whether in a pinch, he'll betray anyone in order to save himself. Mr. Monk, it's a pity you don't work for me. It would give me greater pleasure than I've enjoyed in years to kick you out the door. But then again, that can be arranged here too. I know those members of your board of trustees who pick up most of this school's deficits every year."

Monk laughed, and found it hard to stop. Saddlefield was puzzled—and greatly exasperated at being puzzled.

"You know," the headmaster said, "somebody

very much like you tried to do that to me at another school. And he succeeded. I was fired. But the story got out, and since he had been so crude, using the threat of his money as if it were a nuclear bomb, he became a joke in that city. They called him 'Daddy Warbucks.' There were even some rather unkind editorial cartoons—one of them, as I recall, in one of your newspapers. And that very important man has never been able to shake that name, and the scorn that goes with it. He blames it all on me, of course, and I'm delighted that he does. What also happened—and that I was very sorry to see—was that the school also lost respect. They had to find a hack to replace me because no educator with any self-respect would come so long as 'Daddy Warbucks' dominated the board of trustees."

It was Saddlefield's turn to laugh. Just a couple of short, sharp bursts. "Clearly, Mr. Monk, you are out of your league in the present situation. I haven't the slightest capacity to be wounded by what anyone says about me. As you probably knew, I have been vilified as an utterly ruthless 'press lord' in more cities than you've ever traveled to. I collect those attacks and savor them over wine that my tiny critics will never be able to afford. Indeed, the only time I ever get mildly depressed is when a week or so goes by and *nobody* has attacked me. But I soon manage to do or say something else that greatly enrages more pipsqueaks.

"Now, if Burr should lose 'respect,' as you put it, by your forced departure at my insistence—something I rather doubt because *my* experience with professional schoolmen is that I can buy a far more prestigious headmaster than you to take your place —so what? So what if this place sinks? I'll put Jeremiah somewhere else. You think I give a damn about Burr except for what it can do for my son? Mr. Monk, professionally you are a dead man. You will not remember me as a mere 'Daddy Warbucks.' I will stay in your thoughts as the man who drove you out of education into a more fitting line of work. Being a headwaiter perhaps. You've got the bearing for it. You might go far."

Derek Saddlefield rose.

"Wait," said the headmaster. "There is one more thing I must ask you. If these two boys are expelled, would it bother you at all to find out—a year from now, two years from now—that they were innocent?"

"Find out from whom?" Saddlefield smiled thinly.

"From your son."

"Why would he tell me anything like that? If not now, why a year from now? Or two? Oh, is it remorse you have in mind? We do not breed for remorse in our family."

"Very last question," the headmaster said. "Is it at all possible, from your knowledge of Jeremiah— and you're a man who knows all there is to know about everything that belongs to him—is it possible that Jeremiah has been lying about this?"

Derek Saddlefield looked at the headmaster with contempt. "You want me to make your case for you against my son when *you* have no evidence against him. What a complete fool you are. Are you presenting charges against Jeremiah?"

The headmaster, distinctly uncomfortable, shook his head.

"Then you have wasted my time. And for the last time."

XVIII

"What the hell you going to Chicago for and not taking your horn?" the elder Kelley looked at his son with concern.

"Just in and out, pop," said Major. "I'll be back tonight. This is a different kind of gig. The kind that gets you into heaven—in case there is one. And makes you feel like you done right anyway. It's about the boy. I figure I can help him."

"You're spending that money to help a white boy?"

"Hey, weren't you the one that always told me to take folks as they come, one at a time? 'It ain't the skin,' you used to say, 'It's what's underneath it.' That's what you used to say. All the time."

"I didn't say nothing about spending money on them with white skin," the old man grumbled. "Money comes hard. Being open-minded doesn't cost nothing. They're two different things. If you *got* to spend money, it ought to be on your own kind. They need it a hell of a lot more. Plenty of good black kids to spend on, if you got to spend."

"I promised this boy I was gonna help him." Major Kelley put on his leather coat. "One way I can start doing that, maybe, is to go to Chicago. Can't break my word. That's another thing you used to say. 'If you're not going to do something, don't say you will. But once you say you will, you damn well better.' You gave me them rules. They're good rules. You ought to be proud I made them mine."

"What can you do for that boy in *Chicago?*" The old man watched his son count the bills in his wallet. "It's right here they're going to throw him out of school."

"Newspaper guy out there I used to know when he was working in New York. Cal McDougal. Hung out at the clubs all the time. Used to get smashed all the time, too, but I hear he's off the booze now. He knew the music, he really knew the music, and it was a pleasure talking to him so long as you could understand what he was saying. Anyway, this guy went off to Chicago to be a columnist for the paper Saddlefield owns there.

"McDougal's a gossip columnist," Major continued. "Like he used to be here. That means he picks up all kinds of stuff, including a lot he can't print. I called him up last night, figuring he'd know something about his boss that might be useful, but he didn't want to talk on the telephone. Not about Saddlefield. Stopped me right away. I asked him what if I came to visit him, and he said that would be just fine. We'd talk about the old days. So, it's worth a shot. Maybe he'll open up a little, away from the telephone."

"This Saddlefield," said the old man, "is he part of the Mafia or something, that people are afraid of him?"

"No, pop. He's the kind of cat the Mafia itself doesn't want to tangle with."

Cal McDougal smiled broadly when Major Kelley materialized at his office door. He was very tall, exceedingly lean, and his hair was slate gray, as were his eyes. A picture of Duke Ellington was taped to one wall of his small office and beneath it was a shot of Billie Holiday, a white gardenia in her hair. On his desk were pictures of his wife and two gangling boys, maybe twelve and fifteen. Also, on a far corner of the desk, was a photograph of Major Kelley, his eyes closed, his trumpet raised high.

They shook hands, and then Kelley, before sitting down, went over to the picture of his former self and looked at it closely. "Must have been taken thirty or more years ago. Look at all that innocence."

"You weren't any more innocent then than I was," the newspaper columnist grinned. "The only thing you've lost that you had then is your hair."

They talked for a while about musicians who had died, newspapermen who had died, about some of both who were still living, one way or another. "But you," McDougal said, "you haven't changed at all. Except for that dome. You sure keep in shape."

"A man in my line of work," Kelley said proudly, "has to be in training all the time. Cats like you don't need much breath to type, but to get and hold a good tone all night long, your whole self has got to have *tone*, you dig? Now, the reason I'm here is a boy. Two boys." And Kelley told the columnist about Sam, Rob, and Jeremiah Saddlefield.

"What do you know about young Saddlefield?" Kelley asked.

McDougal got up and closed the door. "To paraphrase Fats Waller," he said, "one never knows who's listening, do one? If the press lord ever found out from one of his shadowy minions—he's got spies on every one of his papers—that someone was talking about his private life, he'd fire the talebearer before you could say 'Dizzy Gillespie.'

"Still"—McDougal leaned forward—"there is gossip. And it travels from some of his staff in his town house in New York to his office there and then to some of us out in the provinces. There's always someone who can't help spreading a juicy story, especially about the rich and powerful and their troubles."

"The boy?" Kelley said. "Jeremiah?"

"A sad story. From what we hear. If you can believe it, he's been stealing almost since he could crawl. From pocketbooks. The maid's. The cook's."

"His mother's?"

"Doesn't have a mother. That is, not at home. She was a drunk. Not before marriage, but after a certain amount of exposure to the press lord's unchanging arctic presence. He's the coldest man I've ever known. I guess she took to the sauce to get some warmth. With all the servants there, including the ones who took care of the child, she had nothing to do but wonder why she was there. And drink some more. Anyway, he divorced her, took the boy, and prevented her from ever visiting him. An unfit mother, the court said. And so she was by then, I suppose. Eventually she disappeared."

"Did Jeremiah steal from his father?"

"Oh, no. Even if he dared, he couldn't have. The elder Saddlefield has always slept with his wallet under his pillow. Not because of the boy, but because the press lord believes that everyone, without exception, is dishonest until proven otherwise. And no one has so been proven yet. I'm told that when *he* was a boy, and quite poor, he slept with a baseball bat beside his bed to protect his valuables from any intruder. I bet he still yearns for that bat."

"Does he know about his son's history of stealing?"

"Oh, yes. Jeremiah has been trundled to an array

of the most expensive child psychiatrists in New York. They all say, from what I hear, that the boy was really just trying to get attention. His father's attention. Well, more than that. His father's love. The press lord was seldom home, you see, traveling hither and yon to gobble up more and more newspapers to which he then had to devote more and more of his time. No time to share for young Jeremiah. So, according to the psychiatrists, the boy stole to pull his old man's coat, as you jazz people used to say. 'Hey, look at me, I exist!' Anyway, Jeremiah, as he got older, expanded his operations outside the house and went in for a little shoplifting. He was caught a few times, but nobody pressed charges."

"Sure," said Major Kelley, "a rich kid steals and he's a sick boy. A poor kid steals and he's a delinquent."

"It's not only that. The elder Saddlefield always saw to it that the shopkeepers were paid back, and then some. Hell, they made a profit from being robbed.

"By the way, I was not being entirely accurate when I said Jeremiah never stole from his father. He never took money—it would have required a platoon of Marines to pull that off—but he did lift various mementoes from dear old dad's study. A small antique clock. A wickedly sharp brass letter opener that, according to legend, had originally belonged to that most fearsome of all press lords, William Randolph Hearst. That sort of loot. Very rare, very expensive stuff. Not like the junk he shop-lifted."

"Did Jeremiah sell his father's treasures?"

"No, they were found readily enough in the boy's closet. You see, the theory is that a certain kind of domestic thief steals something valuable from some-one he likes very much. In doing it, he's acting out a fantasy that what he has just taken is actually a present to him from the owner who really likes *him* very much too. So the thief does not sell what he has taken. He keeps it. You might say he cherishes it. Or so the psychiatrists told Jeremiah's old man. I hear, in any case, that the stealing has fallen off. Maybe the boy has wisely concluded that he will never be able to find his father's affections—since they do not exist, for Jeremiah or anybody else."

"And lying? Does Jeremiah also have a history of lying?"

"Well," said McDougal, "that's part of the process of stealing, isn't it? The boy never admitted any-thing. Not about the thefts from the servants' pock-ets or from the stores outside or from his father's study. For all I know, he didn't even tell the psy-chiatrists either. But they knew from the evidence, which was overwhelming."

McDougal leaned back in his chair. "That's it," he said. "I'm afraid that's all I know." He looked quizzically at Kelley. "You going to try to break the kid?"

"I'm going to try to love the kid," said Kelley, straight-faced.

McDougal frowned. "Somehow, that sounds awfully nasty. As if you're going to love him right into a trap. Still, if Jeremiah doesn't speak up, those other two kids take the rap. And that rap can be around their necks for the rest of their lives."

"You got it," said Major Kelley, rising. "Somebody's got to get hurt in this. No way out of that. Why should it be the innocent?"

McDougal also rose. "Fortunately for me, I'm just an onlooker in this. But—listen, this is none of my business, but I got to say it. Be easy with that boy. As easy as you can. It's hard enough having a block of ice for a father. I mean, that alone can twist you into very strange shapes."

"Yes, indeed," Kelley looked at him. "I recognize that he's still just a boy, a most disadvantaged boy. The thing is to get him untwisted—before he winds up strangling himself. If I can free the innocent, I may be able to free Jeremiah too."

XIX

The wind was stiff and unrelenting, the skies gray, and each of the three, hands jammed in parkas, ears reddening in the cold, stared at the ground.

"Damn!" said Rebecca, her hair whipping around her frowning face. "Damn, damn, damn! It was all I thought about last night, but I couldn't think of anything that would work. He doesn't have any friends, so there's nobody who can get to him. All he has to do is keep his mouth shut, and you guys go to the chair, so to speak."

"This is the first time"—Rob kicked at the iron gate—"I ever realized that while torture is a terrible, terrible thing, there could be circumstances when there's no other way."

"Come on." Sam, having forgotten his gloves, rubbed his icy hands. "Would you really torture him if you could get away with it?"

"Try me," said Rob.

"Stop it!" Rebecca stamped her foot. "We got to *think!* There's no time for this nonsense. Besides"— she turned to Rob—"if you did anything like that, you'd be worse than he is."

"Oh, for God's sake." Rob looked as if he were about to cry. "If I can't just *imagine* something, among friends, no matter what it is—" He banged a hand against the gate. "Ow! I mean, better I fantasize what I want to do to him than actually take that punk and pound his rat face."

"There's got to be a way," Sam muttered. "Isn't there any teacher he's close to?"

"I don't know that 'close' is the word," Rebecca said, "but he seems to spend a fair amount of time in Mrs. Wolf's office. You know, she has a thing about misfits. Either she's studying them or she thinks she can help them."

"That is one great lady!" A fourth voice broke into their conversation. Looking up, they saw Abner Williams, coatless and beaming.

"How long have you been listening in?" Rob said angrily.

"I just now came by"—Williams was still smiling —"and I heard you mention her name. And so I said what I said. Just like, if you'd been talking about Max Roach, I would have said, 'That is one great drummer!' That's all. I'm no spy. Whom I going to spy for? Why Zeke, my brother Zeke, he always tells me, 'If you stretch your ears too far, you're going to lose one of them.' So, have a good day."

"Wait a minute," said Rebecca. "Aren't you *cold?*"

"Will power," said Abner. "It is one thing to acknowledge the temperature. You'd be a fool not to. It is another thing to surrender to it. I let myself feel only so much cold. The rest I turn aside. That way I move free, unlike all you people all bundled up, and I never lose a coat because I don't have one to lose. Not that I *couldn't* have one, I just choose not to be encumbered. Amazing thing, will power."

"Then how come you eat so much?" Rob asked.

"That is my very next project." Abner inhaled a great gust of air with relish. "In three weeks and five days, I'm going to have lost so much weight that if I did have a coat, I couldn't wear it anymore because I'd be swimming in it. You see how all these things work together—if you got the will power."

"Mrs. Wolf." Sam turned to Abner. "Does she take a special interest in Jeremiah?"

"Yes, indeed," Abner said. "She's always looking out for the castoffs, you know. Why, in Zeke's time at Burr, she practically adopted a nowhere kid whom everybody else, including Zeke, thought was the slimiest, trickiest piece of bad news they'd ever seen." Abner paused. "I know why you're asking about Jeremiah and Mrs. Wolf, you know."

"And?" Rebecca said.

"What have you got to lose?" Abner was no longer smiling. "Talk to her. Lay it all out. If anybody can get to that creep, she can."

"Would you come along?" Rebecca asked. "She likes you, even though you're not bad news."

"Sure," Abner smiled. "Also that'll make it an integrated delegation, right? That can't hurt, either, in this day and age. Hey, what the hell is that?"

That was a roar—actually a swift series of roars and growls and anguished, piercing cries, followed by more roars, growls, and screams. They came from a stout, bearded man in his thirties, dressed in a brown three-piece suit, light-blue shirt and dark tie, and carrying an attaché case. The latter, large and sturdy, was occasionally brandished menacingly by the roaring man, who then smote the air with it as if he were surrounded by invisible enemies.

During his few intermittent moments of silence, the man looked like all the other early risers in the neighborhood whom the students were used to seeing hail a cab to their downtown office. Hearing those desperate, raging sounds coming from someone who otherwise seemed so familiar was all the more startling. And scary.

As the man came nearer, they were even more astonished to see that his face was expressionless. It was as if the shouts and growls were coming from a tape recorder he might be carrying. But they were coming from him, all right, his mouth opening in the otherwise frozen face with each terrified, and terrifying, sound. Although he seemed to be looking straight ahead at some kind of blank middle distance, the man suddenly veered to the left on the sidewalk, moving straight toward the four of them standing against the school fence.

Sam jumped in front of Rebecca, and then Rob and Abner stepped in front of her too. The man, now screaming again, lifted his attaché case as he passed them, but he kept on going.

"I've called the police." They turned around to see the headmaster, coatless, on the steps, looking after the screamer. "I saw him from the window," Mr. Monk said, "and then I heard him. Gentlemen," the headmaster said to the boys, "I think we should follow him so that he doesn't hurt anybody."

"Me too," said Rebecca. "I can kick good, if I have to."

The Burr safety squad had not followed the roaring man for more than a block before a police car stopped beside him. Offering no resistance, his cries now soft whimpers, the man got into the car, and they drove off.

"He snapped," Abner said. "That's not the first time I've seen somebody blow a fuse. Last summer, uptown, I saw it twice in one morning. Life gets to be too much, you know. Whatever's weighing on you, crowding you, sitting on your chest—well, finally it gets so heavy, you snap. I really felt sorry for that dude just now. No way anymore he could say how bad things were. All he could do was howl. Like an animal. You figure they can do anything for him?" Abner asked the headmaster.

"I think so. They have medication that will calm him down and then, maybe some psychiatrist will be able to show him a way out of whatever nightmare he's in."

Abner chuckled. But not with humor. "My bet is it's not a nightmare at all. It's real. Much, much too real. I must say, though, it's the first time I ever saw a white man snap. And a white man who looks like he's made it. He didn't get those clothes from no bargain store. Well, Zeke's right again. 'Anybody can snap,' he says. 'Whether you're on top or whether you're down so far you've passed the bottom.' But I bet you Zeke never *saw* a white man break like that. Can't wait to tell him. In fact, if you'll excuse me, I'm going to call him right now."

"I wouldn't be surprised," Sam said as Abner rushed through the front door of the school, "if that psychiatrist finds out that it all began when that poor guy was thrown out of school somewhere for something he didn't do."

"I wouldn't be surprised, either," said Rob.

"Nor I," Rebecca said sharply, staring at the headmaster.

"I hear you," the headmaster said. "But I still don't know anything more than I did yesterday. I

120

wish I did. But neither the world nor this school runs on wishes."

"Sir"—Sam planted himself in front of Mr. Monk—"just between you and us, if you expelled Rob and me, would you believe you'd done the right thing? Would you be sure?"

"This is not the time or the place for me to answer that question, Sam," the headmaster said.

"And when you do," Sam said bitterly, "it'll be too late."

The headmaster looked at Sam, and then walked rapidly away.

XX

Mr. Levine-Griffin was smiling confidently as Sam and Rob entered the headmaster's office. The headmaster, stroking his chin, was seated at his desk, not smiling. He motioned the boys to sit down as he stood up.

"I have come to a temporary decision," Mr. Monk said, "which will be unsatisfactory to everybody."

Levine-Griffin stopped smiling.

"There are no new facts," the headmaster began. "All the facts we do have"——he looked at Sam and Rob——"point to the necessity of your expulsion, because we have never compromised on the issue of drugs in this school."

"Then why not a *final* decision?" Levine-Griffin burst out. "There is no new evidence. You just said so. Everyone has been heard from. Nothing is changed. If you don't expel them, you will be compromising, and that will be a signal to the rest of the student body."

"You haven't heard my decision," the headmaster said. "Its signal, as you call it, is hardly likely to encourage drug use here. But I would much rather that this decision had been final and swift and clear. The problem—the problem for me—is that the facts as we have them so far do not seem to fit the boys as we have them, as we know them. These two boys, I mean. And that forces me to stay my hand, to some extent. I still hope that with more effort, more facts will turn up. On the other hand, nothing new may turn up at all. So I must do something now. I must act on the evidence I do have— short of the extreme penalty."

The headmaster sat down again, his fingers drumming on the desk echoing in the stillness of the room. "Therefore," Monk addressed Sam and Rob, "I am placing you both on probation-expulsion for the rest of the school year. You will continue your classes but if you break any of our rules—*any,* however slight—you will be immediately expelled. In sum, you are on constant probation as to whether you will stay here until June. If you last, and if there are still no new facts to consider in your case, I shall then decide whether you will be able to return the following year. Your conduct until June will be a factor in that decision; but I must warn you that if there is no new evidence by then, it will be extremely difficult for me not to come to the final conclusion that you *are* guilty. I am giving all of us more time, but limited time."

"So much for my credibility as a witness," Levine-Griffin glared at Sam and Rob.

"No," the headmaster said. "There's no question you saw what you saw. But we have no objective witness to what happened *before* you came into the locker room."

"Sir," Levine-Griffin said hoarsely as he moved toward the door, "you are undermining the entire disciplinary structure of this school. It is not only our academic standards that make Burr stand out in this city. And far beyond this city, for that matter. It is the clarity and consistency of our rules of behavior. While parents know that *other* schools have become soft on drugs—with the subsequent softening of their students' minds—they know that Burr stands firm and does not succumb to destructive trendiness. That is, parents *did* know that. Now you have weakened those standards. I bid you good day, sir."

"Probation-expulsion is not exactly being soft," the headmaster said to Levine-Griffin's back.

Sam and Rob got up.

"Sir," Sam said, "we appreciate you're giving us a chance to stay, but this probation-expulsion is awfully unfair, because we didn't do it. But we'd sure rather be in than out, so thank you."

Rob nodded, and then said: "You'll have new facts before June. We're gonna clear our record. There'll be no doubts left when we get through."

The headmaster looked at him. "Be careful that in the attempt, you don't do anything that will make me expel you. I shan't hesitate the next time. Not for a second."

XXI

Once the students' research for the biographical projects was well under way, it was Mrs. Wolf's custom to have her apprentice historians invite their subjects to a class. The lively elders seldom refused, being delighted to find themselves of interest to the young. "I am astonished that you even know my name," one of them said to Rebecca who, in silent truth, had indeed never heard of the person until Mrs. Wolf had announced his coming the day before.

"Why, sure," said Rebecca, pleased at how pleased the white-haired man was. "Who wouldn't know your name?"

And so the class, guided each time by the student biographer in charge of the particular subject —and by Mrs. Wolf—had had a chance to meet a sprightly ninety-five-year-old man who had founded the forerunner of the American Civil Liberties Union during the home-front assaults on free speech in the First World War; the first woman aviator in the Northeast (who complained loudly that if women had been allowed to fly combat missions, World War II would have been over a lot sooner); a gargantuan former professional wrestler with what seemed to be two noses and only one ear; a soprano who claimed to have once sat on Ravel's lap; an alumnus of the CIA who said there was very little he was allowed to say, and proved it; and a retired New York City homicide detective, the hit of the course so far as he reconstructed, in grisly detail, a number of his more fiendishly difficult cases.

From the first, Sam had intended to invite Major Kelley, but he didn't quite get around to arranging a specific date. Forgetful and easily distracted at his best, Sam had become much more disconnected in recent weeks. At night he stared at his homework but his concentration was so shaky that he finished little of it. In school he seemed abstracted much of the time. Unusually silent in class. Unusually careless—even for him—in tests. Not surprisingly, his grades were slipping. Sam worried about them, but mostly brooded about being on the edge of expulsion and about how grossly, how outrageously unfair it was that he should be under this enormous tension. And with all this brooding, all kinds of other things kept slipping out of Sam's mind. Like the invitation to Major Kelley.

But Kelley was persistent in reminding Sam to set up his appearance. So persistent that Sam became quite puzzled.

"Okay, okay," he finally said to Major Kelley one evening, "it's all set up for next Thursday morning at eleven. But why are you coming on so strong about this? You know, there's no bread to this gig."

"As if"—Major Kelley stared hard at Sam—"as if this horn"—he gently patted the trumpet beside him—"were only for hire. As if I were a common huckster, tooting for coins in the marketplace, charging by the note. Boy, I have played more benefits than any musician in the Western Hemisphere. And you—you ask me if I am aware that no money will change hands when I come to your school. As if that would deter me from coming."

"I'm sorry," Sam flushed. "I apologize. I wasn't thinking. Sometimes these days I'm out to lunch."

"I understand," said Kelley. "Nothing more need be said."

"But . . . look, I'm glad you want to come. But I still don't know why you're so anxious to come."

"It is of the utmost importance," Kelley said. "Beyond that, my lips are sealed."

"By whom. Who sealed your lips?"

"We fairy godfathers do not reveal such information."

Having been introduced by Sam, who told the class that Major Kelley was a jazz legend who had influenced hundreds, thousands, of trumpeters throughout the world, Kelley began to tell tales of other giants of black music and of how, in the age of jazz's Camelot, they would meet in all-night jousts that lasted until daybreak—and beyond. Jousts that were called jam sessions.

"Now Coleman Hawkins, he was the King, the first king of the tenor saxophone. He invented it, so far as playing jazz on that horn was concerned. He was the first to make that horn swing, and sing. When he played, the melodies never stopped coming, each one fresh and clear, each one bursting with surprises. And harmonies! My God, Bean—that's what we called him because so much was going on in his head—knew every chord change there was. And he kept finding new combinations, new colors, inside that huge sound of his. There was a man who didn't need any microphone. You could hear Bean clear across town.

"Well, when Bean was in Fletcher Henderson's band, in every town they played, there was an after-hours session where all the musicians from miles around came to hear the local tenors—all the young hornslingers—come up against the onliest Coleman Hawkins. And in every town, Bean put them away, one after the other. He outblew them, he outthought them, he wore them down—and out. He was the King!

"But one night, in 1934, in Kansas City, there was a gang of young tenor saxophonists waiting for him. They were only known around there, you know, but they'd been coming up in fast company because Kansas City, in those days, was the best training ground for jazz players anywhere! The music never stopped in that town. There were so many clubs, and so much music going on in each one, that the air, the air itself, moved in jazz time. And when people went from one club to another, they actually *walked* in jazz time. *Everybody* was swinging."

Sam looked around the classroom. Everyone's attention was raptly fixed on Major Kelley. Rebecca, her chin in her hand, leaned forward, as if in fear of missing a beat. Abner, with a big smile, was taking notes so he could report this historic event to his brother Zeke. And to Sam's astonishment, Jeremiah Saddlefield, clearly entranced, was also smiling. Sam had never figured that a liar and a coward could ever be drawn to anything as open and honest as jazz. Sam was much displeased at this discovery.

"Now," Major Kelley continued, "like I said, whenever Bean came to a town, the young ones would pluck up their courage and go against him. And believe me, it took a whole lot of courage. Like one of them once said to another player in Henderson's band, 'Coleman Hawkins scares me, man.' And that musician, he answered him, 'Boy, he's supposed to scare you.'

"So that night in Kansas City, there were these

young tenors—Lester Young, Ben Webster, Herschel Evans, and some more. And they were scared all right. But not all that scared, because they'd been jousting among themselves, stretching each other, stretching their own selves. Well, the session began after midnight and it went on all night long. Bean against them all. He made that horn tell all kinds of stories, all kinds of ways. He shouted on that horn and he made love with that horn. And he played in keys with all the sharps there was. He loved sharps. And yet, as the light came, the young horns were getting to Bean. But he kept blowing, and thinking, and stomping, and swinging until he was down to his undershirt, still trying to show he was top gun, like he'd always been.

"By the middle of the next morning, though, it was clear that those young guys—and it took *all* those other guys to do it—had cut Bean down. He was out of ideas. Fresh ideas, I mean. But Bean, he would have been there still, figuring that the force was bound to come back, except he had to be on stand with Fletcher in St. Louis that night. So he jumped into his new Cadillac and he drove as fast as that car would go and he burned that car out. Oh, he got to St. Louis—just in time—because Bean, like everybody who lasts in this music, was a professional. And don't you ever forget that. A professional, no matter what work he's in, a professional always makes time."

Major Kelley told more stories, then took out his horn and played a slow, mellow blues. Without a rhythm section, Kelley provided his own pulsing stream of jazz time—the melody floating in the deep, rolling currents of the blues, mostly dark, but with glints of glowing red and sometimes a distant, mysterious blue light.

Then the students, and occasionally Mrs. Wolf, asked questions which Kelley fielded with his customary graceful precision. Like: "What is jazz?"

Major Kelley smiled. "Well, there are a lot of books that try to answer that. Like, you got to swing. But what does that mean? Words won't *do* it. You listen to Count Basie or Dizzy Gillespie or Eddie 'Lockjaw' Davis, and then you'll *know* what swinging is. Those books also talk about 'blue notes' and other things jazz people do with harmony, but you got to *listen* to Ellington and Charlie Parker and Thelonious Monk to know. So let me answer the question by putting it another way. What is a jazz musician? Well, there is a great man, a bass player named Milt Hinton, whom most of you probably never heard of—which shows how culturally disadvantaged you are—and he said it best.

"Milt said that what makes a real jazzman is experience. Not only on your horn. But in your life. He said that unless you've lived a lot, really *lived* —not just existed, not just letting things happen to you—you got nothing to say on your instrument

132

except what you copy off somebody else's records. You see, when we play, what you hear is not some composer's ideas and some conductor's ideas—like in symphony music—but *our* ideas and feelings and memories and anger and sweet satisfaction. So the more we've been through in this life, the more we've got to tell you. You know, some people still say that the only *serious* music is classical music. They even give it that name, 'serious music,' as if jazz is something superficial. Well, let me tell you something. What we play is as serious as our lives. You can interchange one of those fiddle players in a string quartet and nobody will notice the difference. But you interchange one of us in a combo, and it's a whole different group. *That's* what a jazz musician is—he's one of a kind. Like his life."

As the questions continued, Sam was dismayed as Major Kelley took particular care in answering those of Jeremiah. Resentful, Sam tried to catch Kelley's eye to let him know how betrayed he felt. Here this slimy kid had almost gotten him kicked out of school, and would probably succeed yet; but here was Kelley treating him with respect, even affection. But somehow, Major Kelley looked past and over and around Sam, but never directly at him.

When Kelley started to leave, a dozen or so students crowded around him. Some with more questions, others—to Kelley's evident pleasure—with requests for autographs. Jeremiah hung back at the edge of the group, having received a jolting blow from Rebecca's elbow when he had tried to push in at first. Mrs. Wolf had started to say something about that attacking elbow, but Rebecca, with a sickeningly sweet smile, had instantly turned to Jeremiah, saying, "Oh, I am so sorry. Please do forgive me," adding in a whisper as Mrs. Wolf was drawn into conversation with another student, "You stinking rat."

Major Kelley, seeing that Jeremiah was not about to get inside the group around him, made a path through the students as he came over to the boy. "You asked very astute questions, young man," Kelley said. "You have a real feel for the music. You must have been listening a long time."

"No, sir," Jeremiah looked at his shoes. "I don't know very much at all about jazz. Except for some of my father's old records. He gave them to me because he doesn't have time to listen to them."

"A pity," Major Kelley frowned. "A real pity, not having time for music. If you go too long without music, you can wear a hole in your soul. Lack of spiritual nourishment."

"I'd sure like to learn more, sir," said Jeremiah as Sam threw a lethal look at him which, however, did not strike him dead, for all of Sam's ferocious prayers. "How can I find out when you're playing? And where?"

Kelley took a red leather card case from his inside jacket pocket, took out a card, and said to Jeremiah, "Whenever you want to know, just give me a call."

Still ignoring Sam, Kelley waved to the class and went into the hall. His face clouded with jealousy, confusion and outrage, Sam rushed after him.

"How could you, how could you, how could you—" Sam spluttered.

"You are stuck, boy. Give yourself a shake."

"*Him!* That rotten, lousy, vicious Jeremiah. *Him!* You treated him like he was human or something. Worse, like he was special or something. Why WHY? WHY-Y-Y-Y?"

"You know"—Major Kelley was adjusting his coat—"that was a good class. Very bright young folks. And best of all, they knew how to listen."

"You're not answering me!" Sam screeched.

"Have faith, little man. Have faith in your fairy godfather. If you have faith, nothing more need be said. If you don't have faith, nothing that is said will do."

With that, Major Kelley placed a rakish Irish tweed cap on his head, bowed to the guard at the door, and walked into the street.

"I hate jazz," Sam muttered as he turned to go back to the classroom. "Nothing in it you can depend on."

XXII

The old man looked at his son, who was polishing his trumpet, stopping every once in a while to sip from a snifter of cognac. The look was not kindly.

"You're going to sneak into that boy's soul," the old man said, "and sneak out again with his confession. Then you're going to finger him. I don't like it. Means and ends, boy. Means and ends. You use dirty means for I don't care how good an end and you're going to dirty that end. You're gonna prove that two innocent boys are innocent. Now that's fine. Who could say that isn't fine? But you're going to do it by worming yourself into the guilty boy's confidence—pretending you're his friend. Like a snake. Like an undercover cop. Setting a trap. I never thought you would do something like that. You—you who's always talking about being straight with people."

Major Kelley held the horn up to the light, shook his head in dissatisfaction, and rubbed it some more. "You got it wrong, pop," he said. "I'm going to get that sad boy—he's much, much more scared, you know, than he's evil—to confess by himself. I'm going to help him take that weight, that terrible weight, off his soul. That's not being a snake. That is really being a friend, old man."

"I used to know a homicide detective," Major Kelley's father said, "who'd pull that all the time. He could get more murderers to confess than anybody else on the force. He was their friend, he'd tell them, their true friend. He was going to help them feel better, a whole lot better, by letting them take that awful weight of guilt off them. And in time—hours, sometimes days—they finally let it all out. And got sent away for thirty years or something. Didn't make them feel better at all. Made them feel a whole lot worse."

"This is just a kid," said his son. "If he doesn't get straight with himself now, he's going to screw up the rest of his life. I'd do the same thing if he was my own son, wouldn't you?"

"Hmmph," said his father. "My own son wouldn't listen to a word I said."

"Anyway," Major Kelley said, "the only way that boy is going to be able to do this is to first tell his father the truth. That's who he's scared of more than anything in this world. But never more than now. Think about it. It gets out that the press lord's son has been expelled from school for putting two innocent kids' heads in the noose, and all the newspapers that Saddlefield *doesn't* own are going to run that story because he is one hated man. The boy knows that. He knows how humiliated his father would be. That's why it's going to be so hard to unlock Jeremiah."

"So how are you going to do it?"

Major Kelley smiled. "I'm going to do what I always do. Improvise. But they'll be *my* chord changes, you dig?"

The old man shook his head, sighed, and said: "I still don't know why you're messing in white folks' business. Nothing in it for you."

Major Kelley tapped his forehead. "Black brains, pop. Sometimes that's the only kind that'll cut through a problem nobody else can solve. I get a kick demonstrating the power of black intelligence to white folks. Also, I kind of owe it to Sam's dad to help the boy out. We used to be pretty tight back in the time of Fifty-second Street. And I *like* that little Sam. If I'd come up that way, I could have been him when I was that age."

"So what would you have been now?"

"Oh, I don't know," Major Kelley grinned. "Doing something in some office that would have made you real proud of me while nobody else knew my name."

XXIII

Mrs. Wolf, with her firm, coppery skin and lean, unbending height, looked more than ever like an Indian. A still-formidable warrior, despite the long, white hair. Standing against a wall of books in her office, she looked down at Rebecca and Abner, whom she had directed to seats on the couch.

"Let us suppose"—Mrs. Wolf brushed the hair from her eyes—"that your thesis is correct and Jeremiah is the guilty one. Let us further suppose that he has confessed this to me but he has done so under an agreement we made long ago that anything and everything he tells me in this office will be completely confidential. It was a necessary agreement, because otherwise there would have been no way I could have reached that boy. And God knows, he desperately needed an adult he could trust, an adult he could be entirely open with. He's never had that kind of relationship with anybody. Until now.

"Nor," Mrs. Wolf continued in her deep, even voice, "would this have been the first such agreement of confidentiality I have made with Burr stu-

139

dents who have a great need to speak freely to an adult without fear of consequences. And I have never repeated a single word that any one of them has spoken in this room."

"But you would *have* to tell Mr. Monk that the drugs were Jeremiah's!" Rebecca's hands were clenched. "You *couldn't* keep silent when otherwise Sam and Rob would be expelled."

Abner nodded. "With all respect, Mrs. Wolf," he said, "it's not as if you're a priest or a doctor or a defense attorney. If Jeremiah had told one of them he was the guilty one, they wouldn't have to testify against him. But the rest of us—students or teachers or whatever—no matter what promises we make about keeping quiet, we have to speak up for the innocent, right?"

"Thank you for instructing me as to my responsibilities," Mrs. Wolf said icily.

Rebecca was vehemently shaking her head from side to side. "I just don't understand. How *can* you let Sam and Rob be expelled when they didn't *do* it, and you know who did?"

"Ah." Mrs. Wolf's clear green eyes bore in on Rebecca. "But they have not been expelled. And at the end of the year, Mr. Monk will review their records and decide whether they can come back. Obviously, he will decide that they can return, because he doesn't really believe they did it."

140

"But," Abner interrupted, "the expulsion-probation will be on their record."

"It can be expunged," Mrs. Wolf said. "That has happened before, and it is very likely to happen in this case."

Rebecca, her face reddening, rose from the couch. "And this way, you can still keep all your confidences, especially Jeremiah's—that sneak, that liar, that—that criminal! It's awful. It's so awful. It's like you've made yourself into some kind of secret God who decides, all by herself, what happens to people's lives."

"At your age," Mrs. Wolf said with a distant smile, "everything is very, very simple. You will learn otherwise, my dear. My choice would not have been nearly as simple as you think. If Jeremiah had confessed to me, and had then found that the only adult he ever fully trusted had betrayed him, he would have been destroyed. He might even have destroyed himself."

"Mrs. Wolf"—Abner was tugging at Rebecca to get her to sit down again—"what if Mr. Monk *had* decided to just plain expel Sam and Rob—right then? Would you still have kept quiet?"

"*If*," Mrs. Wolf said slowly, "there was anything to reveal, I would have tried to persuade Jeremiah to set the matter right."

"But what if Jeremiah wouldn't go to Mr. Monk

and tell him the truth?" Abner persisted. "What then?"

Mrs. Wolf paused, and unexpectedly reached over and touched Abner on the shoulder. "I don't have to answer that question—for myself, or for you. Because Jeremiah has told me nothing about the affair of the drugs. Nothing. Remember, our conversation this afternoon has been entirely supposition. We have been talking only about ifs."

"But let's keep supposing." Abner leaned forward. "What *would* you have done *if* he was guilty and you and Jeremiah were the only ones who knew it and *he* wouldn't tell?"

"I would have wrestled with the problem," Mrs. Wolf said. "Alone. And it might well be that I would have betrayed Jeremiah. And if I had, I believe I would then have resigned from the staff, because no student would ever again have believed that I can be trusted. As a result, the most vital part of my function at Burr would be over."

"Oh, my God"—Rebecca was walking toward the door—"I can't believe what I'm hearing. I can't believe that *anyone* who knew the truth wouldn't have said so right away. No, I'll take that back. *You* wouldn't, I do believe that. And I'll tell you what else I believe. I believe that Jeremiah *did* confess to you and that you think you're off the hook because Sam and Rob weren't expelled. Well"—Rebecca tossed her hair in fury—"I don't care if you flunk me for saying you're a liar—because you are."

Abner, tensing, expected Mrs. Wolf to hurl a thunderbolt at Rebecca, but the teacher was quite calm. "Actually," Mrs. Wolf crisply told Rebecca, "if you spend more time on your work and less on how you look, you'll get a good grade, my dear. My marking is not in the least determined by personal attitudes, one way or the other."

"You don't deny you know the truth, DO YOU?" Rebecca shouted from the door.

"Young woman," Mrs. Wolf said firmly, "when you show me your license as the keeper of my conscience, I may answer that kind of question from you."

In the corridor, Rebecca was muttering: "Sick. Sick. She's a sick old woman. Thinks she's a goddamn saint. Saint Emma of the Creeps."

"Ego," Abner said confidently as he walked beside her. "That lady get her kicks from being needed by the creeps, and the more awful the creeps she gets, the bigger her ego gets. Boy, I bet she'd pay good money to get her hands on a lonely, lost kid who's actually murdered somebody. Anyway, we drew a blank. A total blank."

"You do think Jeremiah told her the truth?" Rebecca looked intently at Abner.

"Sure. And if that confidence is ever broken, *he's*

going to be the one to break it. You could torture her, and she wouldn't say a mumbling word."

"Why, Abner," said Rebecca, "what a lovely idea."

XXIV

It was a bright Sunday afternoon, but inside the Forever New Dreamland Café, where no sun had ever shone, it was impossible to tell what the weather, or even the season, was. Set below sidewalk level, the jazz club was in a perpetual state of artificial twilight. Also unchanging, on the wall, were jagged caricatures of legendary jazz figures, Major Kelley among them. Nor had the owner changed in appearance for a very long time. Tall, bony, his white hair long and thin, his eyes startlingly bright, Barney Moss, in his seventy-seventh year, stood at the entrance of the room, peering up at everyone who came down the stairs.

"Barney," one of the waiters was saying to a colleague, "always looks as if he's expecting someone to come bouncing back from the grave into this joint. After all, he knows so many people over there by now. And he's convinced that the mighty sound of jazz, if the wind is right, can even raise the dead."

"They said *I* was dead." Barney Moss came over.

"Gone. In the hospital. No pulse. All stretched out
for the last ride. There was a record player in the
room. How could I go anywhere but here without
a record player? So my wife, the one I had then, she
grabs Count Basie's 'One O'Clock Jump,' puts it
on the player, the volume all the way up. The
nurses are running in: 'Take it off! You're disturb-
ing the other patients!' And my wife, she's yelling:
'Look! Look at him! His toes are wiggling! Look,
his head's beginning to nod!' Well, of course. Who
could lie stiff and cold when the Basie rhythm section really starts grooving?"

"Come on, Barney," the waiter smiled, "you
weren't dead."

"Are you a doctor? The doctors said I was dead.
But jazz brought me back. So don't mock. It could
happen to you. Tell your doctor never to send you
to the undertaker until he first plays some Basie
into your ear."

A stringy, hesitant youngster approached Barney
Moss. "Sir, Mr. Kelley said I could come hear him.
I've heard him other places he's played," Jeremiah
continued, "but not here yet. He said to tell you I
don't drink so it's okay."

Barney Moss nodded. "We got Cokes. And since
you're a friend of the Major, no cover charge.
You're a jazz nut, huh?"

"I'm just learning, sir. Just starting."

"*Sir!*" Barney considered the word. "My goodness,

you're either a very polite young man or you're a con artist. I figure the former. Hey"—Moss flagged a waiter—"no check for this young gentleman."

"Thank you, sir," Jeremiah said, and then followed the waiter to a table.

"My man." A strong hand dug into Jeremiah's shoulder, and he turned around to see Major Kelley, as neatly and precisely dressed as ever, with the added festive touch of a red carnation in his lapel. "See you after the set." The trumpeter walked past Jeremiah to the bandstand.

From a loudspeaker near the ceiling, a hoarse voice—Jeremiah recognized it as Barney Moss's—announced: "Ladies, gentlemen and scholars, the Forever New Dreamland Café is proud to present the All-Time All-Stars, directed by the man who, as Duke Ellington said of him, is beyond category —Major Kelley!"

Along with the applause, Jeremiah heard someone say at the table crammed next to his, "Duke said that about *everybody*."

Beside the trumpeter, the all-stars included a short, spry alto saxophonist in his late fifties, and a rhythm section whose members were also well into middle age but who, like the saxophonist and the leader, appeared to have large reservoirs of energy. And confidence. Like his own father, Jeremiah thought. Except that these people weren't bosses of anybody. Not even Major Kelley was giving any orders. As the musicians worked out which tunes they were going to play, it was more like a consultation among equals.

Then, for an hour or so, the All-Time All-Stars swung exuberantly through songs they had resurrected from the resplendent repertoires of Count Basie, Jimmie Lunceford, Duke Ellington, Charlie Parker, and other "giants of American music" as Major Kelley informed the audience. There were also originals by some of the members of the band, including one by Kelley that he had titled "The-When-You-Need-Some-Bread-Before-the-End-of-the-Week-and-Barney-Moss-Is-Hiding Blues."

The owner of the Forever New Dreamland Café, still standing at the foot of the staircase, chuckled.

It was a slow, powerful blues. Big, round, stormy chords sounded deep in the piano; the bassist hunched over his instrument, making it speak with such resonance that Jeremiah could feel the vibrations enter his body. And the drummer, using brushes rather than sticks, made his cymbals sound like a wind whispering mysteries.

The alto player was telling a story on his horn, a story so sad, so hopeless that Jeremiah found tears in his eyes. But suddenly, Major Kelley took the melody, shook it, stretched it, snapped it, and turned the mood into one of defiance. His lean, dark notes stabbed the air, with the rhythm section behind him seeming to loom larger in size as well as sound, for they too were now riding on top of the blues rather than surrendering to it.

On the final chorus, with the whole band in triumphant, soaring flight—the alto now also on fire —Jeremiah felt that he too had become part of the music and an exultant warmth spread all the way through him. It was as if something deep inside him, he wasn't sure what, had been awakened from a long, long sleep. He startled himself by shouting aloud in pleasure, the first time he had ever done that in a public place. Or anywhere else, for that matter.

But when the music stopped, the pleasure, the warmth, the feeling of release—all were gone. Jeremiah was more alone than ever. An outsider in the Forever New Dreamland Café, an outsider everywhere. The music had been so alive, so vibrant with the pride of the players; and he was so without pride in himself. For weeks Jeremiah had tried not to think of what had happened in the locker room, but Sam and Rob had never been out of his mind for long. Yet he had thought time would dull the shame and guilt. But now, right now, with the music gone, he despised himself so much that he wished he were dead.

"I wasn't aware we were playing a funeral." Major Kelley stood by the table. "Hell, I figured we were really cooking up there, but you look like somebody just told you they'd seen the X rays and there's nothing anybody can do."

"That's about it, Mr. Kelley," Jeremiah said, looking into his empty glass.

"Why don't we take a walk?" the trumpeter said. "I like to get out into the air between sets—to make sure it's still there."

When they got to the stairs, Barney Moss looked at Jeremiah, came closer, and looked again. "What's the matter, you sick? I got some Alka-Seltzer somewhere. And aspirin. Better yet, I can get you some hot tea. Listen, that'll fix up anything."

"It's okay, Barney," said Major Kelley. "We'll just get him some sunlight. Remember what that is?"

Moss shivered. "I got a thing about sunlight. A man my age, a man who's lived his whole life in the dark, he gets exposed to the sun, he'll turn into dust. You better be careful too, Major. You're a creature of the night, just like me."

Kelley laughed. "The one thing you can say for Barney"—Kelley turned to Jeremiah—"is that he doesn't go around biting people in the neck. I think."

Up the stairs they went, continuing in silence until they came to a small park, an island in the street. Sitting down on a bench, Kelley stretched his legs, motioned to Jeremiah to sit next to him, and said: "Why don't you tell me what's on your mind?

Something's eating at you, and you might as well let it out before it gnaws a great big hole in there."

"There is something." Jeremiah's voice was so low it could barely be heard. "Something I did. Well, it's more something I didn't do that I should have. Something so awful that, if you knew, you wouldn't want to have anything more to do with me. Nobody would."

"Oh, I don't know." Kelley flicked some lint off his jacket. "I've known murderers and pimps, and even politicians. Why, I shook hands with Richard Nixon once. Ain't nothing shocks me, boy."

Jeremiah sighed. "If—if I tell you, it could only be if you promised not to tell anybody else, *anybody*, because then it might, it would, get to my father and that would be the end of everything. It really would be."

"You got my word," said Kelley. "And mine is the best word there is. I never give up a secret. Once, I knew something that some of the wise guys —you know, the mob—wanted to know. They beat me up real good, even threatened to break my fingers, but I never told them a thing."

"Did they *try* to break your fingers?"

"No, I was working for another wise guy at the time, and they didn't want him to lose any business. So they just hit me everywhere else. Anyway, what you got to say is safe with me."

Jeremiah told him about the locker room, the drugs, whose they were, who got blamed, who should be stripped naked in front of the whole school and driven, naked, into the streets.

"You never told anybody?" Kelley looked at him. "Not even your father?"

Jeremiah lowered his head. "If I told him, he'd never talk to me again. Ever. I've seen him cut people off like that. It wouldn't matter that I was his son. You may not believe that, but it's true. That's the way he is. When my father gives up on someone, it's like that person died. And that's the way it would be with me if I got expelled."

"He'd be *that* disgusted at what you'd done that he'd expel you, too? His own son?"

Jeremiah was startled. "No, no. It wouldn't be because of what I'd done by itself, but because of how it would make *him* look. If the story could be kept quiet, I don't think he'd mind all that much. But it can't be. All the kids would tell their parents, and so the story would get into the papers sooner or later, and he'd be humiliated. You see, for a long time, people have been saying bad things about him for how he runs his papers. That he builds circulation by pushing stories about sex and crime. That he's ruthless with the people who work for him. That he'll twist the news to make some politician he's supporting look good, and that he'll twist the news the other way to hurt some politician he's against. My

152

father laughs at all that kind of criticism. He says they're just jealous because they don't have the guts and the brains to do what he does.

"But"—Jeremiah looked at Major Kelley—"nobody's ever made his private life public, because he doesn't have any—except for me. But now, now they'd say he has a son like one of his newspapers. Tricky, dishonest, no integrity. A son who would betray anyone who got in his way, just like his father. They'd say I was rotten. You have no idea how furious he'd be at me, for having put him in that position. So, like I said, he'd cut me out of his life. Like a leg with cancer in it. Or like my mother."

Major Kelley was silent, his lips pursed, his foot slowly tapping.

"I understand," said Jeremiah as he got up from the bench. "There really isn't anything to say. Thank you for listening. I won't bother you again."

"Sit down, boy," Kelley said impatiently. "We ain't got that much time before the next set so don't waste any of it mucking around in self-pity. You got two choices. One, you go on like you're going. Hiding. Inside yourself. Not being able to stand what's in there. There is nothing in this world worse than that. Nothing. Including your father holding your funeral with an empty coffin. Way you are now, you'd be better off *in* that coffin.

"THINK OF WHAT THE HELL YOU'RE DO-ING TO YOURSELF!" Kelley's roar alarmed a young woman with a baby carriage at a bench directly opposite them. She leaped up and swiftly wheeled the carriage out of the park. Kelley chuckled. "That's a careful mama. Good for her. Nothing more important than that survival instinct. But you, you've got it all wrong. You're choking *yourself,* boy. Get your damn hands off your throat.

"Listen to me"—Kelley leaned toward Jeremiah —"listen real good. If you don't tell what really went down—which is your second choice—you're going to have to keep on living with that. Every day. Every night. It'll be the first thing on your mind when you get up in the morning and the last thing in your head when you're falling asleep. It'll be like wanting to throw up all the time because there's no way you can keep it all the way down. But you can't get rid of it, either. So it'll start to stink, and wherever you go, you're going to think people can smell you coming. I'm talking in terms of years, boy. Now, Sam and Rob, if they get kicked out, well, that's it, man. They'll hurt real bad for a while, but that'll go away. But you, you schmuck, you're giving yourself the worst punishment anybody can have—a life sentence of being disgusting to yourself. And anybody like that can't have no friends, no women, no nothing."

"I don't have any friends," Jeremiah said. "I never had any. Not any real friends."

"All right," Kelley got up. "I've been wasting my

time. There are some folks who only get their kicks from being miserable. And young as you are, you are the champion of them all that I've ever known. I can dig it now. What this is all about is that you're so comfortable feeling sorry for yourself that you've become hooked on it. You're a sadness junkie. Ychhh! People see you coming, they're going to *run* the other way."

Jeremiah, biting his lip, was trying hard not to cry. "You weren't listening. If I do what you want me to do, I'll lose my father, don't you *understand* that?"

"Hell," said Major Kelley, "way you talk about him, I don't see what you'd be losing that's worth anything. I mean the person, not the money. I assume you'd still get some of the Saddlefield bread. Think about that. If you read your old man right and he'd actually cut you out of his life because of the effect on *him* of what you've done—and to hell with *your* life—what's the damn point of caring what he thinks anyway? But why the hell don't you find out?"

Jeremiah, blinking, looked toward the subway. "Good-bye," he mumbled.

"Listen," Major Kelley said, "things could get better. You might get cancer."

XXV

The door to the library, which became his father's office late at night, was ajar, and Jeremiah could hear him on the phone.

"I want him out of there!" Derek Saddlefield was barking. "Circulation hasn't moved for eight months. Don't tell me anything about the bad state of the economy. People will lay out the money for a newspaper no matter what—*if* that front page leaps up and grabs them by the throat. And that's got to happen *every day*. The reader's got to need that paper like a junkie needs a fix. And what he's hungry for isn't world affairs or some Supreme Court decision but blood and sex and political corruption. Raw meat. With everything hanging out, not like the bland stuff on television. That editor you put in thinks he's some kind of Episcopalian minister, so damn well-bred he doesn't want to shock the readers. I want him OUT! Now! Give him his vacation pay and kick him out. I will call tomorrow, and he'd better not be there to answer the phone. You get me?"

As his father slammed down the phone, Jeremiah knocked hesitantly at the door. Derek Saddlefield peered at his son over his glasses. "I'm busy," he said. "Another time."

"It's important," Jeremiah said. "It's very important. I may not have the courage to tell you this at another time."

His father looked at a sheaf of papers, grimaced, and turned his chair toward his son who remained standing. Nor was Jeremiah asked to sit down.

Clearing his throat and shuffling his feet, Jeremiah opened his mouth to be stopped by an angry "Do not *do* that!" The elder Saddlefield pointed to the boy's feet. "You're acting like you're waiting for a tip."

"Sorry." Jeremiah proceeded to root himself to the floor, and looking past his father to a framed headline on the wall—MASS RAPIST SLAIN BY ONE-ARMED FEMALE KARATE CHAMP—Jeremiah, in a dead voice, reported what had actually happened in the locker room at Burr, ending, "They never did anything wrong, Rob and Sam."

Derek Saddlefield, who had been looking through another pile of papers as the boy started, put his hand on them and focused entirely on his son as the story unraveled. When it was over, he kept looking at the boy but from his set face, there was no telling what the publisher was thinking.

"Have you told anyone else?" he finally said.

Jeremiah swallowed.

"*Who?*" his father asked sharply. "You've always been bad at lying, so don't try anything now. Whom did you tell?"

"Major Kelley. The jazz musician. The man I've been going to hear play. But he said he wouldn't tell anybody."

His father rubbed his chin. "Kelley. I remember Kelley from when I used to go listen to jazz now and then. A smooth one. Very smooth. So he's doubling as a priest now? Well, it's done. You told him. But you didn't tell *me*."

"I was afraid. I was afraid of what you'd do."

His father's face was still without expression. "What do you think I should do?" the press lord said. "Wait. What are *you* going to do?"

Jeremiah swallowed again. "It's like a big, smelly lump inside me. And it keeps getting bigger so that sometimes it's hard to breathe. I got to tell. I got to tell the headmaster."

The phone rang. "Not now," his father growled into the receiver. "I'm in conference. Call you back. What the hell do you mean you're going to sleep? For what I pay you, you damn well better stay up until *I* tell you you can go to sleep." And hung up.

"And, sir," Jeremiah said, after taking a breath, "I want to tell the headmaster by myself."

His father kept staring at him. Even when he got

up and started to pace, his eyes never left the boy's face.

"I wish you'd say something," Jeremiah said.

"You don't think I didn't know?" Derek Saddlefield was at his desk again, looking at the phone. "You certainly don't think I'm an idiot. I know when you're lying."

"Then why didn't you tell me you knew?"

"I wanted to see how you were going to handle it. If you'd kept your mouth shut, I would have known that much about you—that in a tough spot, you can cover your tracks. Unlike in the past. Your petty criminal past when you left tracks all over the place."

"Then—then you wish I *had* kept my mouth shut?"

His father lowered his head, seemed to be reading a cablegram intently, and suddenly came up with a smile. "You surprise me, Jeremiah. You greatly surprise me. You didn't surprise me when you first let those boys take the rap. That's the Jeremiah I know. The quivering Jeremiah. The boy who skulks in the shadows. But now this is something new. You're going to speak up, not out of cowardice, but out of a slight touch of courage.

"Mind you"—Derek Saddlefield was pacing again —"I don't give a damn about the morality of this thing. Innocent people get screwed all the time, and clever people get away with whatever they can. But it is true that while most people are either prey or predators—that being the natural order of things—there are always those loonies who have somehow developed a conscience and get hung up on what they call justice. They can be terrible pains in the ass, but I have to have a bit of respect for them. Not on any so-called moral grounds but because they don't bend.

"Some of my reporters are like that. Stiffnecked bastards braying about their integrity. Of course, I get rid of them if they go too far and annoy the advertisers. Or have the gall to criticize me to my face. But there is something in me that sort of admires them. At least they look you in the eye.

"Now you," he pointed a finger at Jeremiah. "I never thought you'd go that route, and I'm far from sure you will. Yet this is the first time in your life that you're willing to take your lumps for what you think is right. A regular Boy Scout. But I kind of admire that, too. Maybe there *is* a backbone there. Where you're heading—which is to take over all these papers when I'm not here anymore because there's no one else *but* you—you're going to need backbone. You've got to get a whole lot tougher, but maybe there is something in you to work with. I haven't thought so up to now, and that's worried me a great deal."

Jeremiah, rubbing his eyes, dropped into a chair.

"Relieved, are you?" his father said. "Well, actually, even though you're going to be expelled, I'm rather relieved, too. You've come through this in better shape than you were before it all happened. But from now on, whenever anything goes wrong, I want to be the *first* to hear about it. You understand?"

"Yes, sir. But nothing will—go wrong. I've learned my lesson."

"Nonsense." Derek Saddlefield took a pencil on the desk and broke it in two. "Unless you spend your life in bed, all kinds of things will go wrong. Some of them won't be your fault. Some of them will be. The thing is: who's in charge, you or all the things that go wrong? So you get slammed against the wall. Just so long as you don't slink down and make yourself a puddle on the ground, you'll come back off that wall. And you'll keep coming back. That's all life is, damn it, unless you get to the point where you have the power to slam *other* people against the wall. Then you'll know you've made it."

"But what if I don't want to slam other people against the wall?"

"All right"—Derek Saddlefield reached for the phone—"enough of this. Got to get back to work. Listen, nobody gets through life without being slammed or being a slammer. Nobody. Even those do-gooders, those loonies with their oh-so-sensitive consciences. How do you think they get their jollies? By slamming evildoers against the wall, that's how. They'd love to do that to me every day, and four times on Sunday. But they can't because I'm too tough for them. And too smart. Much too smart." He started dialing, and said, as if into the phone, "Let me know what that big glass of buttermilk they call a headmaster says."

XXVI

Having finished his confession, Jeremiah waited to be executed.

Walking over to the window, the headmaster stared at the latecomers hurtling past the iron gates. He was still staring when there were no more students in sight. Finally, slowly, he turned to Jeremiah. "This ought to be your last day here. You've done enough to be expelled three times—possession of drugs, perjury, and bearing most foul witness against two of your fellow students."

Jeremiah bit his thumb, and feeling an urge to keep it in his mouth, yanked it out.

"But as you were talking," the headmaster continued, "something came into my mind and would not be pushed out. Absolutely refused to be pushed out. How does it go? 'Joy shall be in heaven over one sinner that repenteth.' I find it very difficult to banish from this place someone who so clearly shows that redemption is indeed possible. You could have gotten away with it. And you knew that. So the only thing you had to gain by confessing was a clear

163

conscience by clearing Sam and Rob. Burr Academy is not exactly heaven, but that's all the more reason to have living proof in this very place that sin is not indelible. It somehow doesn't make sense to expel you for having become a better person, and for having shown the rest of us that, contrary to the comfortable cynical consensus, the leopard *can* change his spots.

"However"—the headmaster so changed his tone that Jeremiah's beginning smile fled—"you will be suspended for the rest of the academic year. That probably will mean you shall have to repeat a year unless, with guidance, you study very intensively this summer. I tend to think though that you would be better off starting with a new class in the fall. That is, a year behind. Yes, that's what you'll do. It will mean a new beginning all the way, including new friends. At least, the possibility of new friends. And when you do return in September, you will be on expulsion-probation until you graduate. If you break any rule, just clean out your locker and don't even bother to say good-bye."

The headmaster rose. "Is there anything you want to say?"

"No, sir." Jeremiah was standing very still. "Except, I appreciate your not expelling me more than I can ever say. And it *will* be a new beginning because, I mean, I feel new."

"To make the obvious even more clear," the headmaster said, "the reason for the harshness of the sanctions, even though they are less harsh than what passes for capital punishment here, is that you did keep two innocent young men in terrible, terrible jeopardy until you finally did come forward."

"I know," Jeremiah nodded vigorously. "You've been more than fair, sir. Much more."

"Yes, I have," Mr. Monk said. "Tell me, what does your father think of what you've done?"

"You mean what I've done today, sir?"

"All of it."

"I can't tell you about the first part, the dope and the lying and Sam and Rob. We've only barely discussed that. But he's pleased that I came forward."

"Really?" The headmaster scratched his head. "Well, he's a complicated man, your father."

"Oh yes, sir. But you see, he likes backbone."

The headmaster smiled. "I see. Then I expect you're involved in new beginnings at home, too."

"I hope so. Sir, I would like to apologize publicly to Sam and Rob. Before the whole student body."

"Oh, you will. I was going to mention that. And on the same public occasion, I shall say a few words about late-blooming backbones. It is a truism, but worth thinking about nonetheless, that those who have known the darkest night of the soul—who have been down so low that there's nowhere to go but up—have something to teach their more fortunate but still vulnerable brothers and sisters.

"But remember, when you come back, your first false step will be your last. At Burr, we may forgive the sinner but we keep a very close eye on him. Well, I can't realistically say, 'Go thou and sin no more,' because you have a long life ahead of you. But I do wish you well, Jeremiah, and I will see you in the fall."

"What are we going to do to celebrate?" Abner, noticeably less bulky than he had been a couple of weeks ago, was hopping up and down in glee.

"I couldn't feel any better than I do now," Sam grinned. "But why don't we get one of them big, big pizzas with everything on it. Two of them. Three of them."

"I'll watch," Abner said sadly. "I got seven and three-quarter pounds to go."

"Oh, we don't need to do anything special." Rebecca's hair seemed to be on fire in the sunlight coming through the corridor window. "I feel like Sam. I just want to keep thinking about what happened."

"I still think," Rob glowered, "they should have thrown the little creep out. For good."

"You're a real sore winner, aren't you?" Sam laughed.

Coming toward them, walking fast and looking somewhere over their heads, was Mr. Levine-Griffin. As he passed, Sam said cheerily, "Thank you, sir."

"For what?" Levine-Griffin, snarling, came to a stop.

"For your apology, sir," Sam said sweetly.

"Now you listen to me." The head of the high school shot out a finger at Sam. "While you may have been cleared by Mr. Monk, young man. I still saw what I saw, and so far as *I* am concerned, you are still technically guilty of possession of drugs. However you obtained them. Had I not happened to be there, I have grave doubts that you would have turned that marijuana in. Very grave doubts. You can be sure that I will continue to watch your every move. You, too." Levine-Griffin pointed his finger at Rob.

"Shall I tell you whenever I go to the bathroom, sir?" Rob's round face seemed to be the most open of books.

"Vulgar." Levine-Griffin spit out the word. "Vulgar, dirty boy. You two are bound to make a misstep, and I shall be there to pick up all the evidence. And next time, it will stick."

"The thing I like about Levine-Griffin," said Abner as the head of the high school bustled away, "is that you can always depend on him."

167

"To be a total horse's ass," Rob interrupted.

"That is precisely what I mean," Abner smiled.

Major Kelley was looking approvingly at a hand-lettered maxim in a thin silver frame. "I found it in some book," he told Sam, "and I copied it out and brought it to this guy around the corner and he did a real elegant job. I think I'm going to make some more, one for each room."

Kelley handed it to Sam who read:

HAVE RESPECT FOR THE INSTRUMENT. THERE MAY BE DAYS IN YOUR LIVES WHERE THAT WILL BE THE ONLY THING YOU CAN CONTROL.

—*Busoni*

"Yeah!" said Sam. "Makes me wish I had an instrument, or anything, that I could always control."

"Not too late, you know." Major Kelley took the framed message and carefully put it on the top shelf of the bookcase. "I know cats who didn't pick up a horn or whatever until they were eighteen or more, and some of them got to be real good. Really in charge. Of course, it doesn't have to be a *musical* instrument. It can be your mind, you know, your intelligence. If you keep it in shape—sharp and clean as a good knife—you'll be okay, even if you never know one chord from another. The whole thing, boy, is to think clear—and let everybody else make the mistakes. Most folks' heads are full of mush. I'd say you had a good start, especially once you learn to dress better."

"Listen," Sam said, "I don't know how you did it, but whatever happened to turn Jeremiah around, it had to be because of you. I know it. I don't know how I know it, but I do. And just saying 'Thank you' is ridiculous, but I got to say it and I got to apologize for thinking you let me down that day when you came to the class."

Major Kelley tried to look modest, but couldn't remember how. "Let me just say that your fairy godfather was on the case. And what he did was to help that boy look into himself. Once he did, that boy couldn't stand what was growing so ugly in there, and he had to clean it out. And the music helped, you know. This music is a mighty powerful force, and it zapped that boy at the right time. Nothing more need be said."

There was a knock, short and peremptory.

"Okay, pop," Major Kelley shouted.

The old man came in, looked at Sam, and said: "So you got free. Free at last, so to speak. You're a lot luckier than most."

"Okay, pop," Major Kelley said in another tone, which meant, "lay off."

169

"You all want to come upstairs?" the old man said. "I got something there."

They followed him up the stairs, and on the kitchen table was a huge round chocolate cake and on its top in red icing: INNOCENT.

"Wow!" Sam shouted. "Wow!"

"For somebody who goes to that kind of high-class school, he don't talk so good," the old man said to his son.

"Pop, you are some special cat," said Major Kelley.

"Boy"—the old man handed Sam a knife—"you cut it. This is your day."

"Mr. Kelley"—Sam was trying not to cry—"I'll never forget this."

"Of course you won't," said the old man. "This ain't no ordinary cake. This cost a lot of money. But," he smiled, "I guess seeing your face when you walked in was worth it. Yes, I do think it was. Now eat! I ain't got all the time in the world, you know, for partying and such. More to life than that, right, boy?" He turned to his son.

"I wouldn't know, pop," Major Kelley took a fork. "I'm just out here playing my horn." And he winked at Sam.